CALLING SEHMAT

Harinder Sikka is currently the group director, strategic business, Piramal Group. After graduating from Delhi University, he joined the Indian Navy. He was commissioned in January 1981 and took premature retirement in 1993 as a Lieutenant Commander.

He recently produced a film, *Nanak Shah Fakir*, which won acclaim at the international film festivals in Cannes, Toronto and Los Angeles. The film won three national awards, including the Nargis Dutt Award for best feature film on national integration.

Calling Sehmat is his first book. It is being made into a film, *Raazi*, by Meghna Gulzar, scheduled for release in May 2018.

Sikka lives in New Delhi with his family.

HARINDER SIKKA

CALLING SEHMAT

PENGUIN BOOKS
An imprint of Penguin Random House

PENGUIN BOOKS

USA | Canada | UK | Ireland | Australia
New Zealand | India | South Africa | China | Singapore

Penguin Books is part of the Penguin Random House group of companies
whose addresses can be found at global.penguinrandomhouse.com

Published by Penguin Random House India Pvt. Ltd
4th Floor, Capital Tower 1, MG Road,
Gurugram 122 002, Haryana, India

First published in Penguin Books by Penguin Random House India 2018

15 14 13

ISBN 9780143442301

Typeset in Adobe Garamond Pro by Manipal Digital Systems, Manipal

Printed at Manipal Technologies Limited, India

www.penguin.co.in

Prologue

In the semi-darkness of dawn the muezzin called out, 'Allahu Akbar, Allahu Akbar . . .' His passionate, full-throated appeal to the Almighty broke the stillness of the new day and slowly Maler Kotla began to stir. As if on cue, the sun gasped through the horizon, flushing the rapidly brightening sky with redness. Yet another day crept into the lives of its residents.

Except for one.

Standing tall and in full glory, the white marble haveli surrounded by lush green lawns had lost its main occupant in the wee hours. For the villagers, especially the women, it was not a mere structure of stone but a symbol of peace, a shrine which they could visit any time and be heard.

With the arrival of the new day, the imposing bungalow of Sehmat Khan quietly slipped into mourning. Tej Khan, the elderly matriarch, and now the only other permanent occupant of the sprawling house, took one last look at her daughter, blissfully calm in death, and quietly closed the bedroom door. Blinking back tears, she made her way to the telephone and fumbled through the painstaking effort of calling up Samar Khan. As soon as she was greeted with a curt, 'Yes?' she said, 'Ammi passed away in her sleep. Come home.' She heard the faint sound of a tortured sigh from Samar's end before he hung up. It was proof of the huge shock he had received. She too put the receiver back into the cradle.

On the other end of the line, Samar Khan was shrouded with a sorrow that seemed to choke his very being. Two days ago, he had come to Delhi on duty from his field station in Amritsar and had requested a weekend leave. He had recently been promoted to the rank of Captain and had excitedly ordered new uniform and badges in which he intended to present himself to his mother. Sehmat had always felt proud and happy to see her son dressed smartly in military uniform. Gasping, he shook his head, trying to clear his mind. He would have to take on the responsibility of a lone surviving son, but it was easier said than done. His mind was in anguish, his vision blurred; tears welled up as if to distance themselves from the grief that ravaged his body.

It seemed a lifetime before Captain Samar Khan could collect himself and call his Commanding Officer, Brigadier Parthasarthy, to seek permission for an emergency leave.

As Samar Khan packed his bags with the essentials needed for the most poignant battle of his life, his Commanding Officer called up that one family member of Sehmat Khan whom she chose to live away from. One of whom no one was aware . . .

Meanwhile, Samar Khan, dressed in his new uniform, got into his white Maruti car and was soon making his way through the barren streets of Delhi to National Highway 1 that would take him to the destination that was still an enigma to him. For once, the young Captain's sensitive mind did not register the vivid tapestry of life in India, as village after village and small and large towns melted away. Instead, his mind ran through a kaleidoscope of images, sounds and fragrances associated with his mother . . . Sehmat Khan.

She was an enigmatic beauty who came into his life when he was merely seven. Ammi, with her serene, almond-shaped eyes and tiny, soft hands; Ammi, with her white chiffon dupatta, edged with fine white lace; Ammi, who made a face when he teased her about her mesmerizing looks; Ammi, who grinned impishly, as she held out keys to the car she had gifted him two years ago; Ammi and her gods, heady on fragrant sandalwood incense sticks; Ammi, who stubbornly ignored him as he yelled at her to shift out from her godforsaken Maler Kotla; Ammi and her soothing, soft voice; Ammi, the most beautiful Indian spy who single-handedly ravaged Pakistan's security system . . .

* * *

Four and a half hours later, turning southwards from Ludhiana, Samar Khan manoeuvred his car through the dusty, narrow roads that brought him closer to his mother. Approaching Maler Kotla, he was struck for the umpteenth time by how little the town had changed over the past two decades. His mother often mentioned that the town had not changed in three centuries. 'The women of our villages must be educated if our country has to grow,' she often remarked. Samar couldn't agree more. A few hours from Delhi, and he observed the changing profile of women, from office-goers to the ones living in abject poverty, becoming slaves to the system. But why did his mother choose to settle down in Maler Kotla of all places? He knew the answer deep within, even if it would never convince him. He remembered Sehmat telling him the history of Maler Kotla and why it was so protected by the Sikhs of Punjab.

The princely state of Maler Kotla came into being in 1454 CE when the Governor of Lahore and Sirhind, Sheikh Sadruddin Sadr-i-Jahan, married the daughter of Sultan Bahlul Khan Lodi of Delhi and was given a cluster of villages in dowry.

In the early eighteenth century, the predominantly Muslim region had witnessed a surge in the population of Sikhs and Hindus, won over by the teachings of Guru Nanak. The Governor of Sirhind, Nawab Wazir Khan, captured the young sons of Guru Gobind Singh, the tenth Sikh guru, after the battle at Anandpur, and agreed to release them on one condition: they embraced Islam. With a conviction that belied their age, Zorawar and Fateh Singh, the nine and seven-year-old sons of Guru Gobind Singh, expressed a desire to embrace death instead.

Baffled and amazed at the audacity of the two young boys, Wazir Khan did not hesitate to order that the proud boys be walled in for slow death. Aghast at his cruelty, Sher Mohammed Khan, the nawab of Maler Kotla and a distant relative of Wazir Khan, protested vehemently and walked out of the court, but his protests were in vain. Sher Mohammed, however, earned blessings from the tenth Sikh guru for his display of humanity and courage.

Since then Maler Kotla had remained under the protective umbrella of the Sikhs and had prospered. Such was the power of the blessings of the tenth Sikh guru that even during the bloodiest of the Hindu-Muslim riots post Independence in 1947, Maler Kotla was peaceful, even as the rest of the nation was nearly torn apart.

Manoeuvring through the sleepy town flanked by the prosperous cities of Ludhiana, Patiala and Nabha, Samar drove into Maler Kotla without even glancing at the vast fields of cotton, aniseed, mustard, paddy and wheat. At almost every passing milestone, he saw one tall structure or the other in the shape of a gurdwara, temple or a mosque, an indication of how deeply spiritual the population was. And almost on each occasion, one thought overpowered his mind, first slipping in insidiously, fading away, and then returning with disturbing vengeance. 'Why can't the rest of the country learn from these people what it means to be an Indian?' he muttered under his breath, as if to give vent to his bridled anguish, his fingers gripping the steering wheel. 'How long will we suffer this caste and religious divide at the hands of our politicians?' He had answers to none of these questions. His only hope was his mother, but she had left him without even saying goodbye.

With this, his thoughts turned to his mother. Ever since he was born, Samar had witnessed numerous problems that she had to face due to the caste divide. Even though he remained a mute spectator on each such occasion, his mind recorded every incident and carried it forward like a recurring deposit in a bank.

The final leg of the journey was the most difficult yet. The intense heat of the summer and the grief in the atmosphere were telling on his handsome features. As his vehicle closed the distance, often reduced to a near crawl because of the potholed roads and dirt tracks, Samar began to feel the same tightening of his chest that had gripped him when he had heard the news of his mother's death. Curious village women eyed him from beneath their bright dupattas. The destination of this white Maruti, bearing a Delhi registration number, was probably obvious to them as his mother was a known figure.

Samar brought his dusty car to a halt in front of the gates of his mother's home and honked for the gardener to open it. Through the bars of the gates, he could see his grandmother sitting on a cane garden chair, motionless, waiting. She looked calm, a fading smile belying the solemnity of grief. No one could tell that she had lost her only daughter.

Samar slowly got out of his car. Somewhere, a brainfever bird was making incessant calls, imploring the summer to hasten. A warm breeze swept through. Samar looked every bit an army man in his crisp olive greens and peaked cap. He looked up and smiled ruefully as the only national flag in the region, perched atop a civilian home, fluttered almost surreally in the sudden swirl of breeze and dropped to inertness just as swiftly.

The natives knew little of Sehmat's past. Many were not even sure of her religion. Yet, she was adored by the women for the manner in which she had fought for their rights and helped them gain their self-esteem. The men too held her in great awe for her far-reaching influence. The Sarpanch, village head, almost feared her because beneath her extremely helpful and meek exterior, he had witnessed her steely resolve, her uncanny intelligence. He was often surprised by the innovative methods with which she solved many of the village issues. She was an integral part of the village panchayat's think tank, someone who had ready solutions to all their problems.

Samar quickly walked to his grandmother and helped her get on her feet. He gazed into her eyes, well aware of the emotions that were building up, waiting for the right moment to pour out. She did not speak. Her smile widened, but quickly changed into a grief-filled expression; rheumy eyes leading to an eventual avalanche of emotional outpouring. Samar had anticipated it all and took her into his strong arms, letting her head rest close to his chest. She broke down for the first time since she had last seen Sehmat. There was little that he could say or do to console his grandmother. The reality had sunk in but the acceptance was yet to come. The soldier in him battled bravely to keep his own emotions from surfacing. He helped her gently sit in the cane chair and pulled another close by, sitting beside her without letting go of her hand. The two sat motionless for some time. Then the old woman looked at Samar with pools of sorrow in her eyes, gently caressed his hair with her trembling fingers and said, 'She is upstairs. Go and see her.'

Samar nodded, and stood up, swallowing the lump in his throat. 'Thank you, Badi Ma,' he said. As he climbed the steps of the house, an aura of familiarity assailed Samar Khan. Every inch of the place echoed with his mother's presence. Even as the life-size portraits of the legendary Bhagat Singh, Sukhdev, Rajguru, Ram Prasad Bismil and Khudiram Bose hung on the outer walls, a selfless, courageous woman lay inside on her bed in eternal peace. She had passed away into the unknown world, unsung, just the way she had wished.

Pushing the brass handle of the door very gently, lest he disturb her peace, Samar stepped in gingerly, throwing away the sure-footedness of military training, only to be taken aback by his mother's shy smile speaking to him from a simple black-and-white picture hanging on the wall.

Sehmat lay on the bed that overlooked the front lawns. The room was airy and open though shadowed by the national flag; the deathly serenity on her face reflecting the shadows of the fluttering flag. Samar was suddenly struck with the awareness that she would never open her eyes and arms to him. She lay covered in a sheet, head draped with a chiffon dupatta, the texture of which was permanently etched on his heart and mind. Wisps of smoke from her favourite sandalwood incense sticks trailed towards the huge windows. Sunlight streamed generously into her room, illuminating her lifeless body and face.

Sehmat Khan had shared her private space with only those who were most dear to her—her gods and her son. Allah, Ganesha, Krishna, Jesus and Wahe Guru were all accorded a place of worship in her sanctum. The other wall had numerous pictures of Samar at various stages of his growing up. Samar watched as the smoke from the incense sticks formed a cloud-like cloak over the metallic figures representing the Muslim, the Hindu, the Christian and the Sikh faiths. A thick wooden plate supported them all, the base of which carried an encrypted message in bold capitals, *Ek Onkar*—there is but one God.

He remembered how proud his mother had been when she had first seen him in his military uniform. 'Respect this uniform, son,' she had said, running her hands on his shoulders, enjoying the feel of the metallic stars on the uniform of the newly commissioned officer. 'And your soul will respect you. Don't be afraid to encounter risks. It is by taking chances that you will learn to be brave. You have a duty towards your nation and you must never weigh it with the materialistic pittance that you may sometimes receive in return. There is no greater reward than to live and die for your country, knowing that you have done your part.'

Tucking his peaked cap under his left armpit, Captain Samar Khan clicked his heels to attention. Tears escaped from his tightly shut eyes as he offered prayers for the unsung heroine of India. He stood proudly as Sehmat would have expected him to. Flattening the right palm at the peak, he saluted smartly. Then lightly touching his mother's forehead he whispered, 'I will, Ammi . . . I will . . .'

His words hung in the room as he slowly walked out.

Holding the banister, he stepped on each wooden stair as gently as he could, looking at the picture frames of the numerous heroes. And as he walked down, a strange feeling gripped him, as if Sehmat were in all those frames, smiling at him, blessing him.

When he emerged through the main door, he looked at the lawns, which were now beginning to fill up with villagers who had come to inquire about their saviour and guide. On seeing him, they rushed towards him. Samar knew most of them personally. He had spent his childhood with them, and respected and loved them for their simple, uncomplicated nature. He could read their expressions and realized it was time to reveal the truth. Without exchanging courtesies with the local politicians who had managed to take their position in the front row, he walked back a few steps and climbed the stairs to the portico. Turning towards the crowd, he folded his palms in a gesture of greeting.

'Dear elders and friends,' he began, 'Sehmat Khan, my mother, was no ordinary person. She was a soldier who lived with only one mission—of safeguarding the country's interest. And she continued to do so till she passed away this morning.' Samar had barely finished when the sound of gasps with looks of disbelief filled the air. Tej Khan who'd been listening intently sat down immediately, trying to balance herself, and shut her eyes, hoping for a miracle to undo the ruthless certainty of nature. As if on cue, the crowd sat down too, stunned at the news of who they thought Sehmat was. Now they were inquisitive to learn more. Their faces reflected sympathy and pain. Seated on their haunches, they inched forward, in order to catch every word. As if divided by a fine line, the women sat with their children on one side of the lawn while the men sat a little distance away.

Their eyes were moist, some were sobbing. Sehmat was their messiah who'd always had their back and had transformed their lives as well as Maler Kotla. The town had transformed into a cleaner place since she'd made it her home. The government machinery had set into motion a mass cleaning process. Perpetually blocked sewers began flowing freely, power supply didn't get interrupted at regular intervals and even local liquor shops adhered to specific timings while conducting business. The local officials couldn't understand her status, but were wary of the mysterious aura that surrounded her. The reason was: Sehmat never came to the forefront. The people in general and women in particular had sensed the importance and the clout that their new next-door neighbour carried about her. They were touched by her politeness, warmth and helpful attitude. Her casual visits to the local markets, residential areas, healthcare centres and schools were invariably followed up by different officials scurrying about to set the prevailing problems in order. Most women were also indebted to her for the money they received in times of need, a debt they never paid back. Sehmat was known for writing off such loans.

The tricolour above fluttered again, taking Samar down memory lane, helping him recall his mother's glorious past, the things he knew first-hand and those that he'd heard only from others. He could now piece together her brilliant life as a spy . . .

1

Sehmat was the only child of Tejashwari Singh and Hidayat Khan, a successful and rich Kashmiri businessman settled in the Valley for many decades. Tej, as Tejashwari was fondly called, belonged to a rich Delhi-based Punjabi Hindu family.

Hidayat and Tej fell in love during her visit to Srinagar. On a cold winter afternoon Tej was walking around the serene surroundings of the Himalayan paradise and, on an impulse, entered one of the boutiques selling pashmina shawls. The beauty of the designs was such that they pulled her towards themselves and soon she was looking through the many that were displayed inside the shop. Tej was wondering what to take back to Delhi for her friends, when a pleasant voice drew her attention from behind.

'May I help you?'

Turning around, Tej found herself looking into the light-brown eyes of a stranger. He was tall, about an inch or two above six feet and wore an off-white Pathani suit. She was struck by his openness and simplicity.

Smiling, Tej asked him about the famed Kashmiri shawls on display. The man moved about the shop with a quiet authority, which made Tej believe that he was the owner of the sprawling emporium. After selecting a few delicately woven pashminas, Tej made for the cash counter to settle her bills.

'Are you visiting Kashmir for the first time, Ma'am?' His voice was now soft and inquiring.

She stopped to respond.

'No, I have come here before and it is always peaceful and soothing,' Tej replied, a slight smile playing on her lips. Wanting to hear more of his rich voice, Tej went on to tell him about her holiday and how she loved the Valley.

Conversation between the two flowed easily. Soon, they introduced themselves to each other. 'I'm Hidayat,' he said.

'And I am Tejashwari. My friends call me Tej,' she responded.

'Can I call you Tej?' he was quick to ask.

'Please do,' she replied, clutching her packet of shawls and moving towards the payment counter. She glanced at the bill, looked at it again, and then at Hidayat questioningly.

'Can't make profit from friends, can I? Hence the discount,' he responded smiling.

Hesitantly, Tej paid the money, thanked her host and headed for the large door of the emporium. A slow warmth filled her heart as she walked out. Somewhere deep inside, she was surprised that a brief meeting with a complete stranger could arouse such strong feelings in her. With a sinking heart, Tej realized that this could be the last time she would see him or hear his alluring voice.

Hidayat stood at the door of his shop with a bemused expression on his face. He could not hold himself back.

He addressed her again, the door chime tinkling in the background. 'Can we meet in the evening? I could take you to some interesting shops to select souvenirs to take back home.'

Tej found her voice caught in her throat.

So this was not the last time she would meet him?

Silently, she nodded. Her heart was wildly beating as she walked away. There was a strange excitement in her heart and a desire to meet him again. She walked some distance, then stopped and turned back to look at the boutique, only to find Hidayat still standing at the entrance, waving at her. She lifted her hand in acknowledgement and moved on. The melodious door chime was still ringing in her ears when she entered her hotel.

That evening, Hidayat rushed through his daily chores of balancing the shop accounts and locking up the emporium. He arrived at the hotel well before sundown and found Tej reading a magazine in the plush hotel lobby. That she was surprised to see him at the hotel was visible on her face. Knowing that her parents would not take kindly to a stranger taking their daughter on a guided tour, she hurriedly went up to him and asked him to wait while she convinced her parents about a short trip to the marketplace by herself. She was able to do that and in a few minutes Tej was back in the lobby, her face slightly flushed.

Slowly the two made their way to the marketplace. They took a leisurely walk around the lake, dodging tourists. Their slow-paced walk was often interrupted by locals who greeted Hidayat, some even asking him for his advice on investing in business and personal matters. It seemed strange to Tej that a man so young was so sought after by not only those his age, but by older people as well. Tej realized that Hidayat was not only respected but also loved by the folks in the city.

They spoke about mundane things at first. However, with each passing minute they became more and more comfortable with each other and the initial awkwardness disappeared. The sun was beginning to set and knowing that it would soon be time for her to go back to the hotel, Tej picked up a few scarves at random, paid for them, and they continued on their way back. She knew she would have to show some kind of purchase to her parents.

In the brief time they spent together, they exchanged much more than conversation. Looking into Tej's eyes, Hidayat could feel that she was not indifferent towards him. His heart was crying out to confess his feelings to her, but he did not want to scare her. Could he dare to tell her how she had captured his heart when she had walked into his shop that morning? Would he frighten her by his admission? What if she disliked him?

Engrossed in conversation, they did not realize that they had walked a long distance and left the marketplace behind. They were now at the far end of the famed Dal Lake that lay blissfully placid, away from the hustle and bustle of the shops. The sky had spread a riot of colours in orange, pink and hues of purple. The trees around it stood like mute witnesses to the beauty and beyond them stretched the hills. A chill in the air added to the romance of the surroundings. Tej had visited Kashmir several times before, but on this occasion, Hidayat seemed to have transformed the lake into a poet's romantic verse. When they parted, they felt as if they were leaving something behind.

That night, as Tej prepared to go to bed, she replayed the day's incidents in her mind. She felt that she had connected with Hidayat at a very special level. Not wanting to lose a friendship that had just begun, she decided to request her parents to extend the vacation. The next morning, over breakfast, Tej convinced her father to stay on in the Valley for a few more days. Then, pleased with herself, she slipped out of the hotel and quickly walked towards Hidayat's shop as was agreed between them the previous day. This was the first of their series of secret rendezvous. When Tej's vacation drew to an end, they exchanged addresses, and Hidayat promised to visit her in Delhi.

It was difficult for them to stay apart, and Tej was overjoyed when she received a letter from Hidayat informing her about his visit to the capital. She began counting the days to his arrival.

Soon that day arrived and they met. From then on, the two met every day and talked for many hours. Hidayat discussed his business and Delhi's fast-paced life compared to the idyllic and simple life in Kashmir. When he left for the Valley, the bond with his lady-love had strengthened. The two continued to exchange letters that seemingly spoke of only the weather and other unimportant topics as each tried to read the unsaid words between the lines and interpret them.

* * *

It was scorching hot in Delhi when Tej and her mother left for Kashmir the following summer. This time around, Tej and Hidayat spent more time with each other, sharing their dreams and aspirations. They had known each other for a little longer than a year and words between them flowed effortlessly, so did their feelings. But both kept quiet and avoided the all-important issue as they were not sure how the other person would react.

Kashmir was alive with colours and birdsong for the young couple. Even Hidayat, who had lived most of his life in the Valley, began admiring Kashmir through the eyes of a poet. The days passed swiftly, and he realized that soon he would have to reveal his feelings. It had to be now or never. So a week before she was due to leave, Hidayat took her for a boat ride around Dal Lake. He was nervous, looking for the right words as he rowed the boat. He looked at her and found her admiring the view, oblivious to what was going on in his mind.

'You love this place, don't you?' he asked.

She nodded. 'I am sad that this vacation is coming to an end.'

'How about staying here forever?'

Tej looked back at him questioningly.

He did not answer immediately. When he spoke, there was a quiver in his voice, 'I want you to stay. I love you and want to cherish our bond for the rest of our lives. Tej, I have loved you ever since you walked into my shop last year. Please don't misunderstand me. Have I scared you?'

Not knowing what to say, Tej's eyes were fixed on the wooden plank at the bottom of the boat. She was stunned into silence.

Hidayat immediately began to feel guilty and wished he had not said what he did. Panicking, he addressed her again,

'Have I said something to upset you? Please don't be angry. It's just that I have never felt anything like this before! Please don't misunderstand my motives. I just know I love you.'

Tej looked into his eyes. Somewhere deep inside she had felt the same attraction and was happy that he finally spoke about his feelings. Clearing her throat, she whispered softly, 'I feel the same way too . . .' Her face turned pink as she blushed, shyly smiling.

It took a lot of self-control on Hidayat's part not to whoop with joy. Instead he looked at her, his face filled with expressions of joy and relief. Taking her hands and clasping them in his, he said, 'Thank you, Tej, for filling my heart with such love!' Tej could only smile in return. She had also begun to worry by then. Being the only child, her parents had pinned lots of hopes on her and had been looking for a suitable match. She was aware of how her parents were focused on finding a match only from the Punjabi community. And here she was, courting a Muslim boy, that too from a trouble-torn state like Kashmir.

Oblivious of the ensuing battle inside Tej's mind, Hidayat rowed the shikara with ease, enjoying the boat ride more than ever before. Each time the oar cut the water at a perfect angle, it gently pushed the boat ahead; the water droplets falling from the wooden blade back into the lake. Seated in front of her, it was impossible to keep his eyes away from Tej's beautiful face. 'I love you,' he said repeatedly until Tej too mustered her courage and acknowledged her feelings.

2

Their love blossomed and culminated in marriage, much against the wishes of their families. Braving boycotts from both sides, the young couple settled down to married life. Sehmat was born after two years and brought along boundless joy, laughter and warmth to the already content household. Conscious of the raised eyebrows due to their cross-cultural alliance, both Tej and Hidayat worked hard to bring up their daughter, teaching and instilling in her the real meaning of secularism.

Being educated and sensible, Hidayat and Tej kept themselves away from undue religious influences and dictates. Neither parent forced any religion on their daughter. Instead, they encouraged her to understand different faiths and appreciate the importance of humanity, integrity, patriotism and honour.

Sehmat grew up watching her parents practise two different religions yet live in complete harmony under the same roof. Neither infringed on the other's choice of religious duties. The room set aside for prayers and meditation had pictures of Mecca, Hindu gods and goddesses as well as other saints and sufis. Sehmat was particularly fascinated by Meerabai's hymns and often joined her mother in singing them.

'God is one,' her parents told her repeatedly. 'And He is not someone who can be summoned by merely holding the Holy Quran and Gita or wearing a tilak on the forehead. He is without a predefined form and resides inside you. He is omnipresent and can only be seen by the purity of one's mind and heart.' Little did she realize at that time that these very values would make her one of the most respected and trusted citizens of her country.

Sehmat was greatly influenced by her father. Hidayat's generosity and positive thinking were legendary in Srinagar. One particular trait of her father, which not only appealed to her but also made her want to emulate him, was his undying love for his *watan*, his country, India. Father and daughter would go on long walks amidst huge chinar trees, one of their most cherished pastimes. Sehmat would listen to her father with rapt attention as they would trek on the narrow pathways in the Valley and learn by heart lessons on patriotism, culture and traditions.

It was during one of those walks that Hidayat, totally consumed by what he was teaching her, stopped abruptly, took her hands in his and said in a voice wrought with emotion, 'We are what we are thanks to our motherland, Sehmat. Nothing can be more disgraceful than to be disloyal to her. I was born here and I must give my best to this soil. When I merge into it, my conscience should be proud of having lived an honest, faithful and grateful life.'

That evening the young Sehmat saw a different Hidayat. She met a man who was passionate and emotive beyond her imagination and respected humanity more than any religion on earth. For the first time in her life she understood what watan really meant to him. This observation was to play a crucial part in her life in the years to come.

As she grew up, Sehmat learnt of her father's role in easing tensions between Hindus and Muslims and his efforts towards spreading harmony between the communities. Hidayat was the final word in settling disputes and conflicts and would always help those in real financial need. Many Kashmiri Pandits would narrate to her incidents where Hidayat's intervention had helped in building bridges between followers of the two faiths.

Thereafter higher education took Sehmat away from the Valley to Delhi, where, besides pursuing her graduation and playing the violin in her spare time, she also learnt Indian classical dance. When she would return to Kashmir for a vacation, she would be regaled with more tales of her father's timely intervention and both communities' indebtedness to her family for spreading peace and harmony in the Valley. The number of such stories increased each time Sehmat visited Kashmir.

Meanwhile, Hidayat's reputation and goodwill as an honest and upright businessman spread far and wide. He was an icon of sorts in the region. His enterprise and large-heartedness catapulted him and his business to the other side of the barbed wire, which, by virtue of the demarcations made post Partition, was now called Pakistan. Hidayat went across regularly to attend to his chores, and add more friends, contracts and businesses to his strength, blissfully unaware that his actions were being closely monitored far away in a plush office in the capital of India. This was the Indian intelligence agency RAW (Research and Analysis Wing). Some senior officials approached him and sought his help to establish an information-gathering network inside Pakistan. Apart from his extensive network, it was Hidayat's legendary love and devotion towards his country that made him an ideal candidate for the purpose. His flourishing business establishments across the border could provide the perfect foil needed for their operations.

Hidayat readily agreed to the proposal even though he was made aware of the risks that his acceptance could invite. He even went a step further by suggesting innovative ideas for gathering information. His merchandise, especially liquor, used to be shipped across the border due to the prevailing prohibition in Pakistan. He proposed to decrease the quantity of each shipment but increase the frequency, thus helping reduce the time gap in retrieving information from across the border. Using his business acumen, he painstakingly spread his network into the cities of Lahore, Islamabad and Multan, and also made inroads into the Pakistani army brass. During the 1965 Indo–Pak war, Hidayat's network became a major source of information gathering. Despite the unsophisticated communication systems of those years, his trusted team devised innovative techniques to transfer huge amounts of confidential documents manually into India, thereby saving the lives of hundreds of Indian soldiers.

While Pakistan experienced humiliating defeat at the hands of the Indian armed forces in this war, Hidayat won the heart and confidence of the Indian government by rendering commendable services. Strangely, he was able to maintain his credibility across the border too, and, despite the defeat, the Pakistani government did not suspect his involvement. Growing from strength to strength, he further expanded his business chain and deepened the penetration into Pakistani army camps by strengthening the supply chain and providing free liquor to the Generals. Prohibition across the border not only added to his profits, it also helped grow his business.

The dawn of 1969, however, brought in its wake a rude shock for the Khans. During a routine medical check-up, a lump in Hidayat's neck was diagnosed to be cancerous. Further investigations and tests revealed that the deadly disease had spread its tentacles beyond control. Tej was shattered by the news but Hidayat seemed unperturbed and indifferent to the development. His mind was focused elsewhere.

Trouble was brewing in the army camps across the border. Hidayat had been steadily receiving reports confirming that the other side was planning a confrontation. He kept grumbling to Tej about how unhappy he was with the bad timing of his ailment. Much to Tej's consternation, instead of paying attention to his failing health, Hidayat put all his energies and efforts into accumulating data and transferring it to the intelligence officers in India.

East Pakistan had by then become a sore point for Pakistan. Egged on by misguided warlords with vested interests, Pakistan's leadership accused India of fomenting trouble in the state. Tej was privy to the new developments, having herself transferred vital information to New Delhi on several occasions, but her husband's indifference towards his illness tormented her.

The very thought of losing Hidayat without making any efforts of treating him medically weighed heavily on her mind. Besides this, watching him in extreme pain unnerved her. Finally, Tej gathered the courage to dial a contact in New Delhi. The government machinery began to move quickly. Twenty-four hours later, when Hidayat walked into his oak-panelled study after namaz, he found two immaculately dressed officials waiting for him. Both men were high-ranking officials from the Indian intelligence. Having interacted with them for many years, Hidayat knew them well. Yet he was surprised by their visit. Manav Chowdhary, code-named Mir, was the head of RAW. It was he who had first approached Hidayat a decade ago for setting up the information-gathering network in Pakistan. Both men had grown to admire and respect each other immensely.

The two men continued to look at each other, neither knowing how to break the silence. It was Mir who finally broke the spell. He reached out to Hidayat, clasped his hand in his own and looked at his old friend. Anticipating the purpose of their visit and picking up on the unsaid words, Hidayat glanced at his wife. He knew what she'd done. A soft flush of guilt reflected on Tej's face.

Mir's voice shook slightly as he struggled to control his emotions. Hidayat was not only an important link, he was a man of honour and a dear friend.

'We have arranged for appointments with doctors in America, Hidayat,' Mir began. 'They will treat you and . . .'

Hidayat cut him short in a polite but firm voice. 'I know my chances of surviving this illness are nil, Mir. And you are also aware of a big disaster that is approaching our nation even as we speak.'

Hidayat withdrew his hand from Mir's, walked to the window and pointed to an object in the distance. The other three in the room quickly looked in that direction. Hidayat's gaze went to the national flag that was fluttering gently in the soft breeze in his neatly manicured lawn.

'Mir, you see that beautiful tricolour? I want to see it flying high when death comes knocking at my door. I have served my mother the best I could and I wish to die in her lap, in my home and definitely not in a foreign country. Let me fade into the corridors of history in peace, in the oblivion of my country's soil and not in an alien land. Besides, there is still a whole lot to be done. While Tej can handle the operations from the Indian side, someone very reliable has to take charge in Pakistan and settle down in the grooves across the border before it's too late. We have little time for anything else, least of all, my health.'

Accepting a cup of tea from Tej, Mir looked at his friend. He knew how important Hidayat was to RAW. He was also aware of the vacuum Hidayat's death would create; to find someone as credible as Hidayat on such short notice was an impossible feat. He wanted Hidayat to get better so he tried to push him further in the hope that he would go to the US for treatment. 'I'm afraid, Hidayat, we do not have anyone who can replace you. Besides, the Pakistanis would not trust anyone in a hurry. They'll smell a rat immediately. In your supervision the operation will remain under the guise of your business umbrella. Even a small mistake at this point would mean the end of the entire network that you have so painstakingly built over so many years. It would also mean grave risks to the lives of the numerous contacts, which we cannot afford at this stage. It is best that we let the matter be put on hold while you go for your treatment. You have done more than your share for the country. Now let us help you fight your battle. I have spoken to the best doctors in the US and they have suggested immediate surgery. We have an outside chance and we must take it.' Mir's voice appeared steady but he could not hide the strain of maintaining equanimity. He had worked closely with Hidayat for so many years, they'd developed trust and friendship, and it was hard to believe that he was dying.

Hidayat seemed oblivious to what Mir was saying and continued to be in a different world. He also knew that his chances of surviving the dreaded disease were slim. At the same time it was bothering him that there was something brewing across the border. He wondered how he could find a solution to all this. He had a distant look in his eyes, his mind racing in circles, searching for a viable candidate to fill his shoes. For years he had painstakingly toiled to build an effective communications network, and he was simply not prepared to let it go down the drain. A solution, however, came to him out of the blue. Hidayat walked towards Tej. He placed his hands on her delicate shoulders and looked into the depths of the eyes of the only woman he had ever loved with so much intensity that it frightened her. Tej, terrified of the consequences of his illness, also instinctively realized that Hidayat had something up his sleeve that might not be to her liking.

Breaking the brief silence, Hidayat said, 'I know it's risky Tej, but it is by taking chances that one becomes brave. You know the gravity of the present situation as well as I do and you will therefore appreciate the seriousness of what is developing in Pakistan. Having come so far, we need to continue with our task and not stop in our efforts to thwart their plans. My illness has come as a cruel shock but we have an even bigger crisis at hand. We can still save hundreds of innocent lives. And to achieve that, we need someone absolutely reliable who can take my place immediately, without rousing suspicion in the enemy camps; someone who can take the baton from me and continue the good work.'

As Hidayat paused for breath, Tej could see that he was struggling with his conscience. Her chest suddenly constricted and her heartbeat quickened. She was almost certain that her husband's next sentence would cause her endless pain. The tension in the room was tangible. Mir sensed it too but was unable to even remotely fathom what Hidayat had in his mind. He thus remained a mute spectator. Hidayat moved closer to Tej with the intention of comforting her from the blow he was about to deliver. In a soft, almost choked voice he said, 'Do you think our Sehmat would fit the bill?'

3

Everyone in the room was shocked into silence. Tej burst into tears. The very thought of pushing her only child into a venture that was filled with danger at every possible turn was heartbreaking. She controlled the sobs that threatened to rack her body and wiped her tears. She felt drained of all strength. She hugged Hidayat and held him in a tight embrace. As a mother she had equal rights but a decision contrary to Hidayat's was bound to inflict enormous injury to his self-esteem and pride. At the same time, it was difficult for her to see her daughter precariously placed at the very heart of danger. She also knew that this decision was not an easy one for her husband. Fighting their own battles within, the two clung to each other motionlessly, fully aware of the pain the other was undergoing.

Dusk had begun to creep up outside the window. The brilliant light was now meekly submitting to the velvety darkness of night.

'Thank you, Tej,' Hidayat continued, supporting her frail body. 'I knew that I could count on you.'

The visitors were stunned into disbelief.

In his entire career Mir had never witnessed a commitment such as the one that was being displayed by the Khans. Speechless, he sank into the plush leather couch and stared in bewilderment at the head of the Khan family. Right then Hidayat walked up to him. Seeing Hidayat approach, he rose jerkily but stood rooted to the spot. He seemed unsure of what to say to the man who was willing to sacrifice his only child, his very beloved daughter, for the service of the nation. Hidayat embraced his old friend. However, when he spoke again, his voice was devoid of sadness and emotions. 'Please look after Sehmat as your own daughter, Mir. From now on, I leave my most precious possession in your care. We have brought her up with a lot of love. We have taught her what we have always believed in. It would be risky for a young woman to take up such a mission but we have no choice. She is the only person who I think can take my place without attracting undue attention from the authorities across the border. And since she is my daughter, it will be readily accepted that she is running the business due to my failing health. Death and danger will shadow her, but the show must go on. We have a long road ahead and we must keep on running till we reach our destination.'

Hidayat's voice had a firmness of purpose to it. Mir could see a man in a hurry to see his mission accomplished, a soldier so possessed by his love for his country that he was willing to sacrifice his only offspring.

Tej's mind was also in a whirl. Looking past the men, she gazed at the darkness that had settled outside the window. She could not visualize her beautiful daughter being thrust into the enemy camp. Sehmat's childhood unfolded in her mind like pictures in an album. The baby she had given birth to, the curious toddler, the animated girl, bubbling with excitement and enthusiasm each passing year. How Sehmat had charmed everyone she met and how she had grown into a beautiful, yet modest young woman!

Tej was aware of the bond the father and daughter shared and was certain that Sehmat would accept her father's decision without protest. But would she be able to stand the vigorous training necessary for the job? What if her secret operations were exposed? Tej shivered at the thought. Her mind raced in many directions but she could not come up with a strong enough excuse to argue. Deep within, the mother in her visualized the worst. And as she did, her heart ached even more.

* * *

Meanwhile, oblivious to these developments, hundreds of kilometres away, in the bustling city of New Delhi, a young woman was sprawled on the bed, her hair spread across it, reading a book. Sehmat was relaxing. She had just come back from college after a gruelling session of dance lessons and wanted to do nothing but read. Sehmat glanced at the alarm clock by her bedside as she turned a page of the gripping book. A soft groan escaped her as she realized she was late for her evening walk.

Swinging her long, shapely legs off the bed, Sehmat slipped her feet into her slippers and made for the bathroom that she shared with her room-mate, Mitali. Both women were classmates and classical dance was a common interest between them.

But that was where the similarity ended. While Mitali was an accomplished dancer, driven by the ambition to achieve fame and recognition, Sehmat danced because it was her passion. Her hands and feet moved in deft coordination with the rest of her body because her soul directed them to. Dance was like a daily prayer for her that made her feel complete.

Though the girls shared the same room, they were not as close as most room-mates in a college hostel are. Mitali was more of an extrovert, while Sehmat was an introvert and took a long time to open up to people. Mitali was of medium height and had a perfect honey complexion; Sehmat was tall and had fair, translucent skin that turned beet red at the slightest provocation. But that she possessed a supreme confidence about herself was evident from her deep-blue eyes, which reflected courage and resolve.

Watching Sehmat was like witnessing poetry in motion. Her peaches and cream complexion, combined with the sharp features common to those from the Valley, was breathtaking. Her movements were effortless which gave an impression that she was gliding instead of walking. To the men who looked at her, she seemed like she had descended from the heavens and did not belong to this world. Her biggest assets were her big, doe-shaped blue eyes; they shone with wit, intelligence and occasional mischief. Quite naturally, Sehmat was the most sought-after girl in college. While men vied for her attention, the women did not know how to react to such beauty and humility. She was not vain despite the fact that she was the most beautiful woman for miles around. If anything, she downplayed her beauty by blending into the crowd. She consciously dressed in simple, loose-fitting clothes to avoid drawing undue attention. She also refrained from socializing and restricted herself from making too many friends.

Many speculated that she had a boyfriend back home since she did not encourage the men. Only her close friends knew that Sehmat did not have any male friends. Looking at her parents, she knew that true love was sacred and it existed. She was also convinced that it would cross her path some day. In her mind she was very clear about the kind of man she would fall in love with. She would see him in her dreams, approaching her and filling her life with meaning, love and strength. She knew he would sweep her off her feet and take her away from the ordinary world to paradise. Though she had a perfect picture of the attributes of her dream man, his face eluded her.

But Sehmat was willing to wait. Her friends often joked about her fantasy, but she believed he would arrive at the designated place at the designated time. Little did she know what destiny had in mind. It was during the annual college celebrations that fate introduced her to Abhinav.

Aby, as he was fondly called by his close friends, belonged to a wealthy and influential Delhi family. Tall and athletic, he looked like a hero from a romantic novel. Women tried to attract his attention but failed. While some admired his drop-dead good looks, there were others who were more attracted to his hefty bank balance. Even though the entire campus swooned over him, he kept to himself and often sat on the last bench of the classroom.

No one, however, knew that instead of taking notes, Aby often penned down his heartfelt feelings in the form of poetry that had only one theme—the beautiful, unattainable

Sehmat. He was in complete awe of her ethereal beauty and often described her as a Kashmiri princess who had lost her identity in an alien city. He loved his princess deeply but could never muster enough courage to approach her. Instead, he poured out his feelings in his poems, which, by his third year in college, had become an impressive collection.

Sehmat often caught him looking at her strangely. While other men made her uncomfortable, Aby's glances were different. His eyes bore into her soul and seemed to search for an answer. Sehmat was instinctively aware of Aby's interest in her. She felt the same, but was determined not to rush anything.

One evening, nearing sunset, Sehmat was taking her regular walk in the park nearby. The orange sun was spreading its hues around the grey-blue sky. She was in her tracksuit, walking briskly. Aby stood unnoticed behind a tree, his usual spot in the park, watching his princess as she walked along her route through the joggers' track. Suddenly, Sehmat stopped and bent over something she had stumbled on. Aby leaned over to get a closer look too. It was a baby squirrel that she was about to step on. She gently picked it up and lovingly placed it next to a bush away from the path of the other walkers. Her eyes shone with love and tenderness, as her fingers delicately handled the creature with ease and comfort. The connection must have been intense, for the baby squirrel didn't show any sign of struggle either.

For Aby, what he saw was surreal. His throat constricted. The fading sunrays reflected brightly on her deep mahogany hair, giving her the look of an angel. He felt as if he were under a spell. On many occasions in the past he had pondered about Sehmat. Her religion was very different from his and could have serious social consequences, since he came from a staunch Hindu family. But at that moment, he put everything aside and became aware of the truth. It was then that Aby decided he would either marry Sehmat or not marry at all.

4

A ll students looked forward to the annual function at
the college and planned extensively for it. One of the
function's main attractions was the dance competition.
Over the years this event had gained popularity amongst
the students. Judged by well-known personalities of the city,
the event had become a symbol of prestige and pride for the
college as well as the participants.

Each year, a committee was set up by the college
administration to oversee the participation and inter-college
representations. Judges for the event were chosen with
great care. The college principal, Ram Naresh Mathur, was
understandably flustered. It was his last year as principal, and
he wanted the event to exceed everyone's expectations. If he
succeeded in creating a mega success of the show, he hoped
his request for a year's extension would be considered.

Mathur sat at the head of the conference table, flanked
by the trustees of the college and their nominees. He took a
quick glance around, noting the different expressions playing
on the faces of the trustees. The slightly built fifty-seven-year-
old principal knew he was no match for the lobby working

against him. For the sake of his daughter, who was in her final year of graduation, he had to work out a strategy to continue as principal for another year. He was known for his straightforward and sincere approach, but he also knew that honesty alone never paid the bills.

To make matters worse, Raviraj Singh, the most powerful of them all and someone he could count on, was absent from this crucial meeting. Many trustees had tried to manoeuvre the admission process to accommodate their relatives and simultaneously mishandled the college funds. Mathur had invariably acted as a roadblock in their schemes and had therefore made enemies within the circle of board members and trustees.

Knowing fully well that most of the trustees were predominantly narrow-minded Hindus, he tactfully chose the theme of the unique love of Radha and Meerabai towards Lord Krishna for the main dance event. Amidst applause and murmurs of approval, he first read out the names of other participating colleges and then the names of participants representing his college. Heading the list of participants was Mitali as Radha and Sehmat as Meerabai. He was about to take his seat when A.V. Shastri, one of the oldest and most troublesome trustees, interrupted. His sharp nasal voice was filled with sarcasm.

'Isn't it a fact, Mr Mathur, that Sehmat comes from a Muslim family?'

Mathur straightened up slowly and thoughtfully. 'Yes she does, Mr Shastri,' he said, his voice tinged with respect and fear. Here was one of the troublesome trustees who could make or break his chance of an extension.

'Then how has she been shortlisted for the all-important role of Meerabai? This will hurt the sentiments of all the students and is quite unacceptable. Many Hindu students could be offended and may take to the streets in protest. We must select someone who belongs to a Hindu family, who can relate to the character of Meerabai. Can a Muslim girl do that? We must shortlist someone else, otherwise we stand the risk of becoming a laughing stock in the eyes of our own people.'

Mathur looked around and, to his dismay, saw that all present were echoing the old man's opinion. Smelling defeat, Mathur was quick to salvage the situation. 'If all the trustees agree with Mr Shastri's views, then we have no choice but to look for another student to play the role of Meerabai.'

'You do? Well, thank you, Mr Mathur. It is not often that you agree to our suggestions and opinions.'

Mathur felt a twinge of pain thinking of Sehmat. He had attended the auditions, and none of the hopefuls came even remotely close to Sehmat's performances. While he was struggling with his conscience, the trustees were wolfing down the remnants of their tea and snacks. There was a collective rustle of papers and scraping of chairs as they prepared to exit the conference room.

Suddenly a young voice, polite but resolute, called out, stopping them in their tracks.

'And why should we do that?'

Standing tall in blue jeans and a T-shirt was Abhinav Raj Singh who had come unannounced as a nominee of his father, Raviraj Singh, and had stood quietly in the corner till then. Besides being an influential businessman, Raviraj was also an important trustee of the college. His ideals, principles and philanthropic activities were legendary. He was respected and feared by almost all in the committee equally. Mr Mathur was hoping to count on him during such a meeting as well as for his own extension.

The committee members were not amused by the young man's audacity in questioning their collective decision. But they were also aware of the consequences of incurring the wrath of the heir to Raviraj's vast empire. Shifting their stance, they welcomed the young man to the meeting.

Aby approached the first available chair. His face was expressionless, hiding the fact that his heart was beating wildly against his chest. His body language displayed no signs of nervousness. But his eyes were cold. They gave the impression that he was present in the meeting for a purpose. Bowing slightly, he glanced at all the members before continuing with his impromptu speech.

'Since when have we started creating cultural differences inside our college? Don't you think, Sir, that by damaging the secular fibre of this very fine educational institution we could be inflicting a serious blow to its reputation? Should we be seen politicizing such matters and risk a divide on religious lines?'

There was a momentary silence in the hall. Those who knew the senior Singh could have sworn that it was the father speaking and not the son. The slow whir of the ceiling fans echoed through the silence but they were not effective enough to dry the sweat on the brows of most of the trustees, especially Shastri's.

Aby's insight was strong, sensible and logical. His words had put the trustees in an embarrassingly difficult position. Shastri gathered himself to make a statement. He knew he could not offend his benefactor even through his son. 'Well, I just made a suggestion, Abhinav. If the committee thinks that Sehmat can do justice to such a vital and glorified role, so be it.' As if stung by a venomous snake, Shastri's voice had lost its power of conviction and influence. Mathur was quick to notice the change and grabbed the opportunity.

'So do we select Sehmat?' The principal's voice had regained some of its authority. Though he sounded unbiased and detached, he secretly felt relieved that a deserving student would be able to showcase her talent. Moments later, the half-hearted grunts from the trustees sealed the decision in Sehmat's favour.

As if on a cue, the principal stood up to conclude the proceedings. His guilt-filled conscience had emerged clean. His voice was filled with traces of victory as he spoke with relief and ease, 'Going by Sehmat's conduct and performance in the past two years, her academic excellence as well as her contribution towards the college's cultural achievements, it is only fair that she be given a chance to enact the role of Meerabai. By selecting a girl belonging to the minority community we would, in fact, be sending a strong and positive message to all about the secular character of our institution. I am also aware that she has performed the role of Radha on many occasions in the past and has repeatedly exceeded our expectations. We therefore need not worry that she will not understand the nuances of the theme or will not do justice to this important role. I am sure that both Mitali Sharma and

Sehmat Khan will do us proud and bring home the coveted trophy.'

After finishing his short speech, the principal looked up for reactions and noticed the raised hand of Mr Bajpayee, one of the trustees. Mathur paused, giving him an opportunity to speak.

'I agree with you, Mr Principal. Abhinav has made a valid point and I second the proposal,' said Bajpayee, in a tone laced with sycophancy. He too owed his existence to Aby's father and did not want to miss an opportunity to drive home his loyalty. The meeting ended with the usual formalities.

Aby decided to remain discreet about his role in Sehmat's selection and walked out of the committee room without waiting to be served tea.

* * *

Sehmat Khan was aware of the notes of dissent from the staunch Kashmiri Pandits. Being a Muslim, she did not expect to be selected for the key role. It was only when she saw the notice pinned on the bulletin board with her name printed on top in bold for the lead role that she jumped with joy. She was ecstatic. A tear escaped her eyes. Her friends clapped and hugged her in a tight embrace. In the short celebration, Sehmat did not notice a smiling Aby standing behind the corridor pillar, taking in every bit of her joy. Feeling elated, he watched her walk away with her friends till she reached the far end of the corridor.

5

Sehmat had seen her mother pray to Lord Krishna and sing hymns of the legendary Meerabai since she was a little girl. Performing Radha's role at school and college was easy. But to be in Meerabai's shoes, and also give a befitting reply to her critics, was a challenge that she was keen to take on. In order to enter into the skin of the character, Sehmat had spent many hours in the college library, reading all the available literature on Meerabai, and rehearsed her part like one possessed.

D-Day approached and with butterflies in her stomach, Sehmat walked on to the stage dressed in the *jogan's*, devotee's, attire: in a pale orange cotton sari, holding a small *dotara*, a two-stringed instrument, in her hand. Mitali entered from the other side of the stage, aptly dressed as Radha. In comparison to Sehmat's simple-looking attire, Mitali was decked out in a bright costume, jewellery and make-up. With folded hands, forming the traditional namaskar, the two dancers faced the overpacked hall. Amidst catcalls and whistles, the audience erupted in loud applause and continued to clap till the two women took their designated places centre stage.

The background music began slowly and swelled into a high pitch as the two dancers picked up rhythm. The strains of the bhajan, devotional hymn, flowed into the hall. Both competitors picked up pace, synchronizing their movements with the poignant lyrics of the song. It was plain for all to see that both the girls were leaving no stone unturned to cast a lasting impression on the audience and the judges.

With her near-professional touch, Mitali let it be known that she was performing to win the competition. The crowd was mesmerized by the delicate movements of her hands cutting the thin air, appealing to Lord Krishna to bless her with his divine grace. Holding a flute, Mitali moved artistically on her toes, encircling Krishna, pushing, nudging and cajoling him to succumb to her demands. She danced with perfection and elegance, swaying the entire audience with her captivating performance. Her colourful costume added to her performance and kept the audience on the edge of their seats.

The challenge was tougher for Sehmat than she'd thought it would be. Even though she was the more graceful of the two, Mitali was flawless in her performance and successfully drew more applause from both the judges and the crowd. But Sehmat didn't give up. Being a natural dancer, her movements displayed an amazing dexterity. She merged with the character effortlessly as the song progressed. As if transformed by heavenly powers, she became the legendary Meerabai who'd devoted all of herself to appease Lord Krishna. She displayed no animosity or jealousy towards Radha whose Krishna enjoyed playing hide-and-seek with her. Unlike Radha who demanded love in return, Sehmat, now transformed as Meerabai, only desired a glimpse of the lord.

Mitali kept pace with her competitor, fully aware that she had the upper hand. She was pitched against Sehmat, a Muslim girl who was playing the part of a larger-than-life character. She had to win, no matter what. Being a Hindu girl from a traditional Brahmin family, she simply couldn't afford to come second to Sehmat Khan.

As the show progressed, Mitali felt something sticky beneath her feet. She looked closely, while maintaining her rhythm, and realized that her toes were covered with blood. Her concentration faltered for a bit. She thought it was blood from her own feet and abruptly stopped her dance to look down. To her relief, her feet bore no trace of injury. Her eyes then followed the blood trail to Sehmat's feet. And what she saw left her dumbstruck. Sehmat's right foot was soaked in blood, which was painting the wooden floor red. Her eyes were shut, oblivious to the commotion she was causing on the stage. The attendants too started lining up on either side of the stage, watching Sehmat in disbelief. They could not muster enough courage to stop her from continuing the performance of her lifetime. Filled with awe and admiration, they stood together, not knowing what to do.

Sehmat had been dancing on a wooden frame on the stage floor, from where an iron nail had protruded due to the repeated stamping of her feet. Her concentration was so intense that she had neither felt the pain nor noticed the blood. Mitali was stunned into disbelief. Looking at Sehmat still dancing with abandon, she felt an overwhelming desire to go up to her and bow down in defeat. Instead, she went to the spot from where the wooden plank had broken loose and knelt down, covering the nail with both her palms. She sat there gazing with admiration at Sehmat's performance. And what she saw from close quarters convinced her that this was divine grace on display and not a competitive dance show.

Volunteers sneaked to the wings of the stage to investigate, wondering what had made Mitali stop dancing. The audience too sensed that something was amiss. Moments later, the word spread in the hall like a jungle fire, making the entire crowd stand up and hold its breath in disbelief. Many stood up on chairs in an effort to take a look at Sehmat's blood-stained feet. But such was the grace in her movements that no one even made an effort to stop the music.

Sehmat continued to dance, her feet stamping the floor in rapid succession. Her body and her dotara swung rhythmically, keeping pace with the music. The volunteers' faces were beginning to change to that of horror. They tried to catch Sehmat's attention, but she appeared to be completely oblivious to the world around her. It was as if Meerabai had reincarnated as Sehmat Khan, taking the sarcasm, taunts and abuses of society in her stride, calling out to her beloved lord to take her into his fold. There was passion in her movement, love on her face and pleading in her expressions. Her attire was simple, but her movements were divine and soothing, touching the hearts of everyone present in the packed auditorium.

Sehmat's performance was at its peak as the music reached its full crescendo. Her braided hair majestically swayed to her lithe movements as she ended her dance by kneeling down.

She had tears in her eyes, not because of her injured feet, but for the love of Krishna to whom Meerabai had given herself.

Her eyes were shut, as if taking in the blessings that were being showered upon her by an unknown, heavenly force. She opened her eyes to deafening applause, only to realize that she was on the college auditorium stage. She hurriedly turned towards Mitali and then towards the audience before bowing in acknowledgement. It was then that she noticed her bloodstained feet.

Mitali was smiling at Sehmat with tear-filled eyes. She was defeated hands down. But in her defeat she had won the applause of the entire audience who had instantly recognized her gesture. Mitali walked up to Sehmat and held her in a tight embrace. The hall broke into another round of applause. The roar grew louder as the two stepped towards the seated judges and bowed before leaving the stage.

When Sehmat reappeared on the stage to receive the trophy, the glow on her face was brighter than the gleam of the trophy. Sehmat requested Mitali to stand with her while receiving the award. The two dancers stood together, hand in hand, holding the trophy high with pride. The crowd continued to applaud well after they had left the stage. It was evident to all that both the girls had emerged victorious. They had won something more valuable than a mere trophy. Goddess Radha and Meerabai had been united with their Lord Almighty.

The only person who did not join in the frenzy was Aby. His eyes were transfixed on the face that had bewitched him for so long. Her enthralling act touched him as deeply as most of her other attributes. He had never seen her dance before but had imagined she would dance beautifully. Her performance erased the fine line of religious divide and strengthened his conviction that she was an exceptional woman, worthy of taking on as a life partner.

While the spectators in the hall continued chatting about what they had witnessed, Aby slipped away unnoticed. His mind was now racing in all directions, looking for a means to get closer to Sehmat. He was determined to remove the social barriers of caste and creed that had kept him away from her. He had now begun to dream of a life with his Kashmiri princess. Shutting his eyes ever so briefly he murmured and then amidst another round of deafening applause emerging out of the hall, looked skywards and said, 'I hope you will hear my prayer, dear Krishna.'

Sehmat and Mitali were invited to the backstage room specially meant for guests immediately after the performance and showered with more praise. With his decision of selecting Sehmat vindicated, the principal felt elated. He put his right arm around her shoulder and introduced Sehmat to the board members and the judges. The same trustees who had earlier wanted Sehmat out of the competition were now giving her compliments. It was then that she learnt from a repentant Shastri about Aby's intervention in ensuring her selection. Touched by Aby's gesture and emboldened by her victory, she decided to personally thank him.

* * *

Later, holding Mitali by her arm, Sehmat walked back with a slight limp to her hostel room with her bags and costume.

Filled with a surge of trust in her new friend, Sehmat shared with her what Shastri had said about Aby.

'You should meet him, Sehmat. You are aware of the fact that he is attracted to you, aren't you?'

'I don't know, Mitali. I have seen him look at me at times, but I haven't given it much thought,' Sehmat said hesitantly.

Mitali placed her hands on Sehmat's shoulders. 'I do not know how you will react. But everyone in the class is aware that he is madly in love with you. In fact, it is common knowledge in the entire college. But are you attracted to him?'

Sehmat flung herself across the bed with a sigh, 'I do not know, Mitali. He is indeed handsome, and I think a decent man too, but there are times when doubts overcome me and I cannot decide.'

'There is only one way to find out,' Mitali said and picked up a bunch of roses from one of the bouquets that were presented to her. Handing them to Sehmat, she winked, 'You can thank him. What better way than to say it with flowers? And I will help you look for this handsome young man.'

6

The next morning, at the college, Mitali's detecting skills were stretched to their limits in trying to locate the elusive Aby. She finally found him in the library and rushed to Sehmat. However, on hearing this, Sehmat became so nervous that it looked like she was about to break down.

Mitali tried to encourage her, 'Go on and meet your hero. I would like to listen to your conversation, but right now I need to get back to my classes. I've missed so many for this dance!' And with that, Mitali left an agitated Sehmat to her own devices.

Sehmat hesitantly walked to the library and looked around for Aby. Something in her told her that since he was behind her success, it was only fair that she thanked him, no matter how awkward she felt. She peered into the semi-darkness of the library. For as far as her eyes could see, there was no sign of him. She felt disappointed and was about to turn away, when she spotted him seated at the far end, his head buried in a large coffee-table book. Slowly she inched towards him, thinking about what she would say and how she would start the conversation. As she approached his table, she found him engrossed in a colourful book titled *Meerabai*. He did not notice her till she was standing in front of him, and when he finally saw her it looked like he had been struck by lightning. He stood up hurriedly, took her hand gently and shook it with tenderness and care.

'That was the best dance performance I have ever witnessed in my life. You were simply superb. Heartiest congratulations.' Words did not flow easily. Aby looked visibly shaken yet pleasantly surprised by Sehmat's sudden appearance.

Sehmat smiled in return. She could see that Aby was dumbstruck. Sehmat quietly extended the bouquet. He graciously accepted the roses from her and then pulled up a chair for her. Sehmat sat down self-consciously, but noticing his discomfort decided to do the talking.

'How can I thank someone who doesn't even want to acknowledge what he has done for a person unknown to him? Please accept my deep and heartfelt gratitude for helping me out. Without your support I could not have achieved the greatest moment of my life. Thank you so much. I hope I will be able to reciprocate your kind gesture some day.'

Sehmat's soft, comforting words lifted Aby's spirits. He made up his mind then and there to tell her about his feelings without making a pretence of friendship. He smiled at her. It was the most tender smile Sehmat had ever seen. He stood up and gently placed the roses on the table. The moment between them was electrifying. All the students present in the library looked inquisitively in their direction. Aby looked into Sehmat's eyes for the first time. The warmth in them was encouraging enough to dispel his hesitation. Drawing closer to her, he bent slightly to look straight into the hypnotic twin pools of the deepest-blue eyes.

'You have never been unknown to me, Princess. We have never met formally, but you have always been in my thoughts and in my heart. I have known you right from the day you first entered the college. I wanted to speak to you but there was never a right moment. You are different from the rest. The way you carry yourself, the way you speak . . . You have always been a part of my dream and the centre of my poetry.'

Sehmat got up from her chair and stood right in front of him. They were so close that they could feel each other's breath. Aby paused for a moment, his eyes locked on to Sehmat's. Even though he was speaking softly, all ears in the library were tuned to pick up every word that was being exchanged. But this was his moment and he was determined to open his heart. It was now or never. 'What if I say I like you, and that I love you? That I have loved you right from the moment I first saw you and that I feel incomplete without you?'

It was Sehmat's turn to be shocked. She was unprepared for such a reaction from Aby. She had always tried to stay away from relationships. Now his declaration of love had thrown her off. She knew nothing about Aby, his family or his background. She stood looking at him, taking in every feature of his face, every fleeting expression. She thought about the times she had caught him looking at her with admiration and passion. Suddenly she had a feeling of déjà vu and the realization knocked the wind out of her lungs. The man standing in front of her, professing his love for her bore a striking resemblance to the man in her dreams! That is why she had been drawn to Aby in the first place. He was the man she used to think about. When did she fall in love with Aby? Why hadn't she realized that she was in love with him till this very minute? She was grappling with her own feelings and trying to come to terms with how she felt.

Meanwhile, for Aby, Sehmat's silence was deafening. He could not understand what Sehmat was thinking. What if she rejected him? The feeling would haunt him forever. Fearing a refusal, his heart nearly stopped beating.

Sehmat decided to let her emotions take the lead. She had waited so long to feel this way and was now ready to take a chance. She shook her head in an attempt to clear her feelings. Tears began streaming down her face as she barely whispered, 'Yes.'

'Yes, what, Sehmat?' he asked desperately.

Sehmat looked at Aby. Her eyes held the emotive response that he was hoping for, but Sehmat went a step further. 'I love you too. It just took a very long time for it to sink in.'

Relief flooded Aby's face. As if guided by an invisible force, his hands met hers, her fingers clasping his palms with passion and excitement. The warmth flowed easily between them but the two lovebirds preferred to stay quiet, letting their expressions do the talking. After a few moments, Aby broke the silence, 'When you shook your head, I thought you were going to deny us a chance.'

Sehmat smiled shyly and rested her head on his shoulders. If it were a dream, she did not wish to be woken up. Her feet were bandaged but her heart had healed, completely.

Their moment was interrupted by a sudden noise around the table. Onlookers, relieved that the suspense was over, were thumping the desks and cheering the new couple, who had just exchanged vows of commitment in their presence. Aby helped Sehmat wipe away her tears. Her face had turned pink. She was blushing, smiling and crying all at the same time, leaving telltale marks on Aby's shirt for all to see.

'We'd better leave this place or we will be fined for creating a ruckus!' Aby said taking her hand firmly in his and escorting her out. They made a remarkable pair— the beautiful, delicate Sehmat, hand in hand with the handsome and protective Aby. Together they walked towards Aby's car.

Once in the car, Aby turned to her and said, 'I hope this is not a dream. I promise you, Sehmat, that I will always love you. You may think it is too soon for me to say this, but I have felt like this since the time I first saw you.'

Sehmat was touched by his words. She wanted to savour every moment of it and not worry about the uncertainties. She remembered what her mother had once said: 'Love can only happen once and when it does, your heart will tell you that it is the one true love. Allow that to happen when it does.'

She voiced her thoughts to Aby, who smiled back at her with a lopsided grin, enjoying the warmth of her head resting on his left shoulder. After hours of aimless driving, Aby turned the car towards her hostel. 'Let's get you to your hostel before the warden decides to throw you out,' he joked good-naturedly.

'These two days have been truly the best days of my life, and I owe them to you, Aby. First, my chance to perform and now, your love . . .' Sehmat sighed.

'Now that the lady has had enough excitement for one day, her chariot drops her at her palace so she can rest and wake up fresh in the morning,' Aby said with a smile as he applied the brakes. He opened her door gallantly, and Sehmat got out and walked towards the hostel gate. As she turned around to wave at him, she saw a sad look cross Aby's face. She rushed back to him. Touching his cheek, she tried to lighten his mood. 'We will be meeting each other every day, Aby. Who knows, you might get tired of seeing me so often.'

'Ah, the lady has a sense of humour,' Aby said, brightening up. 'See, I picked the most amazing woman on earth. But for now, return to your palace or the stepmother will banish you from her kingdom.'

Still smiling widely, Sehmat ran to her room.

Mitali, with her head propped on two pillows, was reading a book. As soon as she saw Sehmat, she lowered her book and gave a mischievous wink. 'That was quite a long thank you, don't you think, Sehmat?' she teased. The word about Sehmat's meeting with Aby in the library had spread like wildfire. But Mitali knew she would hear the entire story in detail, first-hand.

Sehmat went up to Mitali and hugged her. 'You'll never guess what happened, Mitali. I had gone to convey my thanks and . . .'

'I know, I know, your love story is quite the hot topic at the moment. But I won't let you off with an incomplete version. I want the entire story right from the moment I left you till the time you came waltzing into this room. We still have half an hour before dinner. So why don't you shower and change first?' Mitali looked at Sehmat's foot, which appeared to be fine except for a slight swelling.

Sehmat dutifully obeyed. Clutching a fresh change of clothes, she disappeared into the bathroom, to emerge from it ten minutes later, scrubbed and refreshed. Her foot was beginning to throb but her heart was far too joyous to worry about the pain. While Mitali took her shower, an exhausted Sehmat lay on the bed, her eyes closed, thinking of the day's incidents. By the time Mitali stepped out of the bathroom, Sehmat was fast asleep.

Mitali looked at her. She had witnessed Sehmat's reaction on a few occasions when issues pertaining to women's rights had been discussed. That was when the shy, reserved maiden from the Valley had donned the mantle of an activist and spoken passionately on issues relating to the freedom of women. But here she was, vulnerable and delicate, lost in her dreams. Her innocent face radiated with an amazing glow. There was a sense of deep satisfaction in her body language as she slept in complete peace, perhaps dreaming of Aby.

The Meerabai in her had found her Krishna at last.

7

Sunlight streamed into the modest hostel room, kissing the face of the girl sleeping next to the window. Stretching luxuriously, Sehmat woke up and glanced around to find Mitali, her room-mate, still asleep. She slipped into her bathroom slippers and decided to go to the hostel mess for her morning tea. She went downstairs to find that the cook wasn't there yet. Sehmat decided to stroll around the hostel grounds as it was a pleasant morning.

The air was fresh and the birds were flying about, in search of scraps of food. A pigeon scampered in front of her, focused on something on the ground. Impressed by the lush green surroundings, the lone bird soon began marking his territory on the vast grassy carpet by pumping air into his neck and going around in circles. As if on cue, more pigeons joined in, challenging its authority and starting a beak fight in the process.

Sehmat sat on the steps and began observing nature at its best. Her face broke into a smile, which soon turned into a loud giggle. It was not the pigeons' tap dance but the memory of how Aby had admitted his love for her at the library the previous day that made her laugh. What she could not see was the radiance on her own face, a natural glow which no cosmetics in the world could have brought out.

Even as Sehmat was engrossed in her thoughts, the cook had come back to the kitchen. Seeing Sehmat at peace with herself, he couldn't help admiring her. She was blushing, he noticed, but didn't understand why. But he cared for her and was pleased to see her in such great spirits. He approached her, holding a hot cup of tea on a tray.

'Good morning, Miss Sehmat. I heard about your excellent dance performance yesterday. Congratulations. May you always come out with flying colours!'

Sehmat looked at the aged chef and smiled, 'Thank you, Dheeraj Kaka. That's sweet of you. By the grace of God, it went off very well. Your good wishes helped indeed.' The cook was touched by her humility.

Extending the tea tray towards her, he pointed to the sky and remarked, 'He does not make simple and warm people like you every day. To be in Meerabai's shoes is no mean feat. And which is why he selects special people for special roles.'

Sehmat gracefully accepted his compliments and the tea. There was a big lesson in his plain words, she thought. Taking a quick sip, she raised her eyebrows in appreciation and requested another cup. The chef obliged. Holding both cups, she began climbing the stairs to her room. On the staircase, she bumped into a few early risers who were making a beeline for their morning tea as well. While Anjali, a second-year student, congratulated her, Helen, her classmate, laced her sentence with sarcasm, 'You seem to be the lucky one, winning two trophies in a single day!'

Sehmat simply smiled in return and continued climbing the steps. She pushed open the door to her private sanctuary and found her room-mate still asleep. Mitali's magnanimous gesture during the competition had removed the wedge of mistrust between them and had brought the two dancers closer than ever before.

'Wake up, sleepyhead, it is the room service,' she said. Getting no response, she continued, 'Oh, don't you want to know all the details of yesterday. The offer expires in ten minutes and after that no matter how much you plead, I won't tell you anything.'

Mitali sprang up from her bed as if jolted by an electric current. Smiling and yawning almost at the same time, she accepted her cup. The mischief in her eyes showed that she was ready and wide awake. 'If love makes you get me a cup of tea each morning, I pray you never fall out of it.'

'Just this morning, dear. I woke up early and decided to be nice to you,' quipped Sehmat. She then picked up her pillow, put it on her lap and sat down on Mitali's bed to regale her with details of the entire incident, ending with the comments from Helen on the staircase.

Mitali dismissed Helen's comments with an elegant wave of her hand, fully aware that Sehmat was capable of standing up for herself. 'Those girls are jealous for a reason. Both of you are stunning creatures. Aby has been the heart-throb from the moment he joined college. Then you walked in and many of us began to wonder when you would cross paths. It was obvious to all that Aby was in love with you but we were never sure about your feelings for him.' The girls chatted for another hour before preparing for another day.

Sehmat dressed slowly and carefully as if it were her first day in college. The woman in her had begun to take charge.

They were greeted with both pleasant and unpleasant looks all through the long corridor. Bemused, the girls giggled their way to the classroom. Sehmat looked around for Aby amongst the few students who had arrived, her eyes scanning the rear bench that he usually occupied. Mitali was quick to notice her disappointment. 'Oh, so from now on, the lady would prefer to sit at the back for a panoramic view and take lessons on love rather than attend the lecture?'

Sehmat smiled back meekly but did not respond. Holding her by the elbow, Mitali climbed up the steps of the class and walked to the last row of benches. The classroom began to fill up as more students arrived. The two took the fifth bench from the rear. Mitali looked at Sehmat's disappointed face and said, 'He'll come. Men often need more time to get ready. After all, it is his first day too!'

The first lecture on Shakespeare dragged endlessly, even though it was Sehmat's favourite subject. Walking up and down the stage, the professor described Romeo's eternal love for Juliet. He described the scene when Juliet appears in the balcony and Romeo looks at her. 'Thou . . .' he began the dialogue of Romeo. He was so engrossed that his hand went up comically as he enacted the scene, leading to bursts of laughter from the students. But Sehmat was not paying attention. With her head resting on her arm, she was waiting for her Romeo to arrive. Her eyes were closed, and she was blissfully unaware of the comic melodrama that was taking place in the class.

'Thou!' she heard again. Only this time the voice sounded familiar to her. She opened her eyes and listlessly turned around to see Aby sitting behind her, grinning from ear-to-ear. 'Thou,' he whispered again, winking at her. Sehmat blushed a pretty shade of pink and turned her face towards the professor. Almost at the same time, the gong sounded, signalling the end of the lecture. The classroom emptied out in minutes except for the three students huddled together as if engaged in a serious group discussion. Mitali was centre stage, acting as the group leader, giving sermons to Aby.

'From now on, Mr Romeo, a simple "thou" won't do. I expect you to pick Sehmat up from the hostel, drive her to college and be by her side for the rest of the day, each day! Though I sincerely wonder what would happen if you two decided to skip a few classes. The sky surely wouldn't fall or would it?'

Aby smiled in return. 'Thank you, Miss Mitali, for bringing us together. All I can say is I am deeply indebted to you.' Sehmat noticed the gratitude in Aby's voice as he spoke to Mitali. *He is different*, she told herself. She closed her eyes momentarily and thanked God in a short prayer. Mitali broke the silence, 'It was a pleasure indeed. You two beautiful people deserve each other. It had to happen one day. Now will you two please get lost?'

The trio left the room together, only to be separated again at the car parking. Mitali bid them goodbye and stood watching Aby's car roll down the long driveway towards the college gate. Sitting by his side, Sehmat had inched closer to Aby. The two indeed made an inseparable pair.

* * *

Their love blossomed with each passing day. It was rare for either to be seen alone, except in the classroom. Even while attending lectures, Sehmat fought hard to focus on her studies.

Aby maintained his backbencher status. But his voluminous collection of poetry on Sehmat began drying up. Instead, he passionately admired her and occasionally exchanged paper slips, commenting on her clothes, hair and their meeting plans. Every note carried a couplet or two, often leaving Sehmat spellbound with his selection of words. Sehmat dedicatedly kept the tiny notes as prized possessions, neatly pasting them in a scrapbook at the end of the day. These notes soon became her favourite pastime and she pored over them whenever she found herself alone.

They met regularly even as the annual exam fever gripped the college. Aby promised to carefully study her notes but found it difficult to focus. Somewhere deep within, he was worried about the approaching summer vacation that would take his sweetheart away from him.

Perhaps he had a sense of foreboding of the impending storm in their lives.

On the day of their last exam, Sehmat had barely stepped out of the hall when an unknown person approached her. He introduced himself and gave her a sealed envelope. Thinking it to be one of Aby's pranks, she looked at the envelope carefully and found the sender's name at the bottom. She was taken by surprise and hurriedly opened it and read the short note. Mir had requested her to fly back to Srinagar. The envelope also contained an air ticket for a flight that was scheduled to depart the next day.

Sehmat instinctively realized that all was not well at home. Shortly thereafter, she was sitting in the principal's room, talking to her mother over the phone. Aby sat by her side, maintaining a studied composure. Tej tried her best to allay her daughter's fears and pretend that all was okay, but failed. Aby too couldn't do much to bring cheer to her face. They dined in silence, after which Aby dropped her at the hostel, only to return a few hours later, this time to take her to the airport.

In a way Sehmat felt guilty. She hadn't really thought about her parents in these past couple of weeks. She wondered if she'd been unusually selfish in being absorbed in love. The guilt and the worry began to consume her. Aby was patient but also worried, 'Please call me as soon as you reach home. If you need me, I'll take the next flight. Are you listening, Sehmat?'

Sehmat was lost in her own thoughts. She merely acknowledged Aby as she left him. On the flight, worry consumed her in the form of various thoughts. *What could have happened for them to send for her like this? Her father hadn't spoken to her, was he okay?* She sighed tiredly and looked out of the window as she knew she would have to wait till she got home.

* * *

Once at home, Sehmat slowly became aware of what was happening. She came to know about her father's ailment and spent a day crying as she thought about the possibility of him passing away. Her mother was patient with her, talking and explaining things till late in the night. Sehmat told her about Aby, and the two found solace in their tears. Tej told Sehmat about the possibility of her becoming a part of the intelligence-gathering network across the border. Even though she had dreaded talking about it, she explained how it would happen.

'Aby is but a small sacrifice,' she said. 'Your father has toiled hard and taken grave risks for the sake of our country. He would like you to take over from here and help in controlling the other end, especially in light of the growing battle cries from the overconfident Pakistani Generals. Besides, we have known the Sayeeds for decades. Iqbal is a very fine, well-mannered and educated boy. You'll be very happy and safe,' she said. Sehmat was to be married to the son of a Pakistani Brigadier, Sheikh Sayeed, in a bold move to understand the operation being carried out against India.

Deep in her heart, Tej felt a stab of pain for her daughter. This is not how she had imagined her daughter's marriage. She knew Sehmat would obey her and do as she was told. But she also realized the consequences of sending her only daughter into the enemy camp.

Sehmat found the shock of losing both her father and Aby unbearable. She wept and sought explanations from the Almighty in the privacy of her room. If it were a test, she would rather fail than be away from her family and Aby, she argued with him.

Swinging between anger and despair, she sought answers that no one could provide. The dark night reflected her state of mind: a sense of doom reverberating all around the stillness. It was an omen of things to come, Sehmat thought.

Her thoughts flew to Aby, who was waiting for her. Her anger was directed towards her fate. She couldn't let her father down but she also wanted to be with Aby. And there was no middle ground.

* * *

Hidayat Khan had a long talk with his daughter in the study the next day. He talked at length about his love for the country and how he had managed to set up the network which now needed someone to take over. He explained how he couldn't trust anyone other than her. Sehmat watched the emotions come and go on her father's face. She could literally feel the pain he was going through, and she understood the gravity of what he had handed over to her. *How could she let him down? How could she walk away from this?* She would be risking the entire operation if she defied the ground rules. Her family's honour was at stake. She would have to make the supreme sacrifice and, without looking back, bury the memories of her true love in the sands of time. That was how it would be, and she had to decide very quickly.

Sehmat took the entire day to think about her decision. Her parents did not disturb her or try to influence her but there was anticipation in their eyes. She was restless during the night too. The next morning, Sehmat made her way downstairs to tell her parents of her decision. Instead of servants of the house attending to their chores, she was met by neighbours and friends of the family assembled in the drawing room. For a moment she was disoriented. With a sinking feeling, she rushed to her parents' room. There she saw Tej kneeling by Hidayat's side, weeping softly. Hidayat was lying on his usual side of the bed, with his eyes closed.

Fearing the worst, Sehmat quickly reached her father's side. Sensing what her daughter was thinking, Tej shook her head. 'He suddenly developed a complication this morning. The doctor has been in to see him and has administered some injections. He needs to rest,' she whispered. Something was different about Sehmat today. There was no trace of tears on the young woman's face whose life had taken such a drastic turn, without being given a chance to react or recover.

Later, Sehmat talked about her decision. She would do as expected—get married three months later—but not before making a trip to Delhi. Her parents were relieved but also worried for her. With a heavy heart they let her go to Delhi, one last time.

The first person Sehmat met was her soulmate. Aby listened to her in shock and bewilderment as she outlined her destiny. Sehmat trusted him completely and, against the strict advice of Mir, unveiled the reasons and secret behind her hurriedly planned marriage to the Pakistani Captain. 'My father has sacrificed himself for our nation, Aby, and the least I can do is give him peace as he approaches the last phase of his life. Besides, it would be an honour to be able to serve our motherland,' she said, talking about her decision.

Aby wasn't convinced. Not only was he going to lose Sehmat to another man, he also foresaw serious consequences to her personal safety. 'Do you realize that you are not cut out for such a dangerous operation? Are you even remotely aware of how spies are treated if they are caught?'

Sehmat did not respond. She saw the unbearable pain he felt in his eyes. Since she had decided to be betrothed to another man, she was honour-bound to end her relationship with Aby. But her heart was not responding. It was instead revolting, forcing Sehmat to merge with Aby's soul. For the second time in her life, she allowed herself to be led by her emotions. Moving closer to Aby, she whispered, 'Please hold me in your arms. Who knows what will happen tomorrow. I'll live with the memories of your love for the rest of my life.'

Their faces streamed with tears as they clung to each other. Aby was finding it hard to breathe. He could not imagine his life without Sehmat. Her tinkling laughter, her smile and her sweet fragrance were engraved in every pore of his being. But now he had to let go. He looked into her eyes and said, 'I have loved you, Princess. I always will. Remember, I am here for you. All you need to do is reach out to me. And no matter what, I'll be there.'

Sehmat nodded through her tears. Scared that another moment with him would weaken her, she pulled away gently, wiped her tears and walked away from his life, and hers too.

8

Hidayat passed away a month later. He died as he had wished, watching the tricolour fluttering in the gentle breeze, his wife and daughter by his side.

In a short span of time, Sehmat lost the only two men she had ever loved. She was drained of all emotions. What mattered now was only her mission, to make her father and the country proud.

Sehmat spent the next one month inside the Red Fort in the heart of the capital, where she underwent intensive twelve-hour training at the hands of intelligence officers. The agents, hand-picked by Mir, trained Sehmat in the art of setting up and using micro listening devices for the first two weeks. The second half of the month was even more gruelling, as she learnt to physically handle small arms, explosives and detonators.

Sehmat displayed an amazing and uncanny knack for espionage techniques and worked extra hard so as to exhaust herself by the end of each day. However, she failed to remove Aby's picture from her mind and spent hours poring over her scrapbook. Those were the only moments that made her emotional. By the time her training came to an end, she had become an expert on numerous spying techniques. When Mir met her at the end of the month, he looked at her proudly. The girl was her father's daughter all right.

A month later, Sehmat was married to Captain Iqbal Sayeed of the Pakistani Light Infantry at Lahore. Iqbal's father, Sheikh Sayeed, was a serving Brigadier in the same branch and was known to be close to the top brass. He had very carefully cultivated friends in high places as he had climbed up the military ladder. Shrewd and calculating, he'd even gone to the extent of getting his elder son, Major Mehboob Sayeed, married to the daughter of an Army General. This in turn ensured that the Brigadier was favoured during the crucial promotion period. Given the Pakistani army's penchant for martial laws, its Generals were known to value personal loyalties over rule books, codes and ethics.

Even though Brigadier Sayeed was mediocre in strategic planning, he made up for it by being smart and quick on the uptake. He understood the fact that those who displayed brilliance also posed bigger threats to the top brass and were therefore quickly sidelined. To save his skin, he preferred to play the role of a 'yes man'. Whenever summoned for advice, he first researched what his superiors wished to hear and then advised accordingly.

He and Hidayat Khan had studied together at Lahore College and were close friends. Post Partition, Sayeed had helped Hidayat expand his business. In turn, Hidayat had assisted Sayeed in arranging expensive liquor and fancy gifts for senior army officials in his parties. Marrying his son to an Indian girl was a risk, but such was Sayeed's influence in the army that Hidayat was sure of him overcoming any consequent problems. Sayeed had another reason to be happy. He had an eye on Hidayat's business empire of which Sehmat was the only heir.

Mir knew that Sehmat would be safe with the Sayeeds. He also saw a bigger role emerging for the Indian intelligence. He had failed in persuading Hidayat to withdraw Sehmat from this dangerous course, so he took it upon himself to ensure the safety of his friend's daughter. He deputed his most trusted and efficient officers in the Indian Embassy at Islamabad and spread his network around Sehmat to provide her with an alternate escape route as and when the situation demanded.

After the wedding ceremonies, Sehmat settled into the new environment quickly. It was important for her to overcome her past and focus on her assignment. The open and friendly atmosphere at the Sayeeds' distracted her from the memories of Aby to an extent. But at the same time, she found it difficult to adjust to the very thought of living in an alien land that was becoming more hostile to her own country with every passing day.

Unlike most Pakistani families that lived behind the conservative walls of a religious mindset, the Sayeeds had a modern outlook. Their women could speak up in front of male members and were free to make significant decisions on important issues. Almost every male member of the family was either serving in or had retired from the Pakistani army. Consequently, they enjoyed enormous political clout. It soon became obvious to Sehmat that the Sayeeds were more feared than respected in the social circles they moved in.

Sehmat lost no time in acquainting herself with the traditions and customs of her new household. As a quiet observer, she made mental notes about the family, its dynamics and internal politics. Being the youngest daughter-in-law, she was showered with love and attention by all the family members and servants, which helped Sehmat establish her own identity and position in the household. The Sayeeds appreciated the fact that despite her personal loss, Sehmat was only spreading good cheer all round. She was always smiling no matter how heavy her chores were.

Sehmat soon earned the confidence of the men of the family on the business front as well. While conducting her first business meeting, she not only showed maturity but also skilfully negotiated the deal, leaving both her husband and father-in-law in complete awe. A large shipment of spices belonging to an importer was confiscated at the Karachi Port. Unable to pay the high penalty, the importer refused to pick up the consignment. Sehmat made agreements with a few buyers at a profit and paid for the entire consignment. This brought a windfall profit to the Sayeeds' home. With good money pouring in, Brigadier Sayeed began to look up to Sehmat for advice on various issues, including his own official ones.

Sehmat remained diligently focused, in spite of the smooth sailing. At every opportunity, she searched for safe locations to instal her listening devices. Two large photo frames in her father-in-law's room were her favourite and most important spots. Each afternoon, while the men were at work and the women napping, Sehmat painstakingly and meticulously mounted the tiny pieces of equipment and concealed them the way she was taught. These devices could then be controlled by her from the safety of her bathroom through a portable unit.

The bathroom soon doubled up as an operations room from where she could send an SOS message or even make an emergency call. Using microscopic headphones, she also became a mute listener to the meetings that the Brigadier held at the haveli with his deputies.

Though Mir had categorically warned her from doing so, she went on to instal and commission the Morse code equipment and, under the cover of the running water, transferred vital messages to the other side of the border.

She gave no reason for anyone to suspect her activities. With her charm, love, openness and friendly behaviour she had won the hearts of the Sayeeds. The only fly in the ointment was the elderly Abdul, a servant of the Sayeeds who had served them for over twenty years. Behind his thick grey beard and wrinkled face, Abdul had a set of piercing eyes that missed little. Abdul did not trust Sehmat. Even though she tried, Sehmat could not win his trust and confidence, which made her extra cautious all the time.

Abdul served the Sayeeds with fanatic loyalty. He had come to be treated as a member of the family from an ordinary household servant. On one occasion, he had risked his life to safeguard that of his master's. A snake had attacked the Brigadier while he was taking his morning walk on the front lawns. Abdul had then shown exemplary bravery in picking up the reptile and tossing it away, but not before getting bitten by the venomous snake. Abdul had survived the attack but the Sayeeds carried the debt of gratitude on their conscience and treated him as a respected elderly member of the family.

Abdul had nurtured in his heart an irrevocable hatred for all Indians. And he had his reasons. Post Partition, while he had managed to escape to Pakistan, his entire family had been slaughtered in front of his eyes during the Hindu-Muslim riots. Having unsuccessfully voiced his opposition to Captain Iqbal's marriage to Sehmat, Abdul could never bring himself to repose faith in the new bride.

The Sayeeds were aware of Abdul's deep scars and his prejudice against Indians. He held the entire nation guilty for an act of violence that had made him understandably bitter. But the Sayeeds had hoped to erase his painful memories. In the bubbly, innocent and fun-loving Sehmat, they were sure that they had the right prescription to heal his wounds. Sehmat too looked forward to an opportunity to remove some of the bitterness in his heart, and also win his trust.

Her first chance came during the annual inspection of units under the command of her father-in-law. Amir Khan, the General Officer Commanding (GOC), was known for his ruthlessness. He wasn't a man to cross swords with. Since the GOC was in the last leg of his long service, his high-handedness and haughtiness had reached its peak. For Brigadier Sayeed, it was time to press all buttons to ensure that his units met with the highest standards.

Pacing up and down the lawns of his palatial haveli, a nervous Sayeed was at his wits' end thinking of various ways to appease the GOC. Sehmat, who had been observing her father-in-law's quandary, saw a golden opportunity to prove herself worthy of his confidence and trust.

On the pretext of going to the Jama Masjid, a public mosque some distance from their house, Sehmat covered herself with a burka, got into her car and drove away. Before entering the mosque, she slipped into a telephone booth and hurriedly dialled a number she was made to memorize as part of her impromptu training by Mir.

'Yes,' came a sharp voice from the other side.

'This is Romeo 221022 Zulu. Lieutenant General Amir Khan, GOC Light Infantry. Urgently need complete details, family background, hobbies and weaknesses. Shall call tomorrow.' There was a momentary silence at the other end. Sehmat instinctively knew that she had taken the First Secretary by surprise. The recognition and recovery on the other side, however, was quick. 'Okay,' came the short reply.

Sehmat replaced the receiver and picked it up instantly. She dialled a dummy number to ensure that her call could not be traced and placed back the receiver. During her short training, Mir had repeatedly impressed upon her not to leave anything that could be traced back.

Sehmat went back to a different telephone booth the next day and was soon smiling under her burka as she heard the brief on Amir Khan. 'Thanks,' she said softly as she replaced the handset and repeated the drill. She then drove straight to her husband's office and, dismissing the guards with cheerful smiles, perched herself on the thickly cushioned green sofa.

Captain Iqbal Sayeed was issuing instructions to his men when he was informed of his wife's arrival. Amazed and somewhat shocked, he rushed to his office to find Sehmat closely observing the map on the wall and encircling landmarks in red ink.

'What are you doing here at this hour of the day, Sehmat? And why are you messing with this map? This is no time for jokes, you know. The GOC is inspecting units in fifteen days and I have no time to even breathe. Abba Huzoor will be very angry if he comes to know about your surprise visit in such a time of emergency.'

'I am going to meet Abba Huzoor, but wanted to see this map before I did. So will you please drive me to him right now?' There was a soft cajoling play to her voice as she drew imaginary circles on the thick leather of the sofa with her long shapely fingers.

Iqbal was speechless. What could his wife possibly want to say to his father that apparently couldn't wait? She knew too well that the Brigadier was tense and in ill humour and yet she was trying this stunt. But before he could say anything to her, Sehmat had already left the office and was opening the door of Iqbal's car which was parked in the driveway, while simultaneously ordering the driver to take her to Brigadier Sayeed's office.

Iqbal barely managed to sit inside the car as it sped to its new destination. And before the confused and visibly shaken husband could start with his round of rapid-fire questions, the car came to a halt at Sayeed's office.

Sehmat, who was without a burka by now, kept herself a pace ahead of Iqbal. Bowing slightly and gently, acknowledging the salutes of the amused guards, she stood at her father-in-law's office door and knocked softly.

'Abba Huzoor, hum andar aa jaain? [Respected father, may I come in?]'

There were about fifteen officers seated around the table who instantly stood up and smiled at Sehmat. Her unexpected presence had added colour to the dull and drab room. The Brigadier wasn't pleased though, and, with great effort, stopped himself from snapping at his daughter-in-law.

'Of course, please come in. It is indeed a pleasure to see you. I hope all's well?' he said and simultaneously gave a hard stare to Iqbal who tried his best to wear a not-guilty look and feigned ignorance. Escorting Sehmat to the sofa, he turned towards his officers who quickly scrambled away from the room after exchanging pleasantries.

Holding her father-in-law by his arm, Sehmat walked him to the wall that had a large-scale military map. 'This is where the inspection will begin and end, Abba Huzoor,' began Sehmat with confidence and poise, pointing her finger at the lake site earmarked on the map. The Brigadier listened to her in complete silence for the next half hour. As she began to reveal her ideas, his tense face began to relax.

Escorting her back to the car, he said, 'I had heard that brides bring luck to their in-laws. I am more than convinced of that now.' Iqbal could only marvel at his wife's intelligence and guts. She had not only come up with an amazing plan, but also had the nerve to barge into his father's office unannounced and get away unscathed.

* * *

For the next two weeks, Sehmat and the Sayeeds' trusted servant, Abdul, carried fish feed to the lake and dropped it at a particular point. While the rest of the family wondered what was going on, Sehmat smiled under her breath and waited for the final day.

On the day of the inspection, the GOC, along with the guard of honour, was walking back with his deputy when the Brigadier, as instructed by his new tutor Sehmat, made his move. 'Sir, we have made a slight change in the drill. Tea with officers is being held at the lake site in order to give you a picturesque view of the core headquarters.'

'But why did you do that, and why did you not inform me before?' roared the GOC.

'Sir, the men felt that with your vision, foresight and ideas, the unit could go a long way in terms of future planning. They were sure that you could see what we all can't and wanted you to have a macro view of the entire establishment. Besides, Sir, I happened to notice that the lake is loaded with possibly the finest fish waiting to be hooked. If you like, maybe you could spend some time fishing, while the officers assemble at the lake site?' suggested Sayeed.

The Brigadier's heart was in his mouth, while Amir Khan considered the political correctness of the situation. But like all anglers, Amir could not resist the lure of fishing. He was at the fag end of his career and was in a position to make a minor change in tradition, after all. 'Well Sayeed . . .' he continued, 'I don't like sudden departures from the standard drill. But now that you have done it, let's go ahead. Besides, one has to respect the feelings of our men. By the way, are you sure there's fish out there? Why haven't I heard of this lake before?'

While the officers sipped tea at the lakeside, their GOC busied himself in counting the number of fish he had caught within half an hour of dropping the hook. Like a much-desired trophy, he lifted the largest fish and, exclaiming with joy, looked at his deputy, 'I say Sayeed, have you seen her size? She weighs nearly a ton!'

Sayeed was about to say something when he remembered his daughter-in-law's words. Looking philosophically towards the lake he said, 'Sir, I don't know much about fishing. But I know for sure that it is caught not with the hook but with the power of one's mind.'

Sayeed's response was music to the GOC's ears. His eyes lit up. This was exactly his philosophy and how rightly put! He glanced at the assembled officers who were only waiting to break into applause. Feeling on top of the world because of the massaged ego, he turned towards Sayeed and said, 'I didn't know you are so deep into books, Sayeed. I say, I am impressed, very impressed.'

'Thank you, Sir, but this calls for celebrations. This lake too demands to be honoured in the annals of history. It would therefore be appropriate if you could address the men from this very site.'

'I think that is a very good idea. I am very happy to see your units in such great shape. Your men must be congratulated for all the efforts. Tell them no more inspection. They can relax now and I'll meet them in the evening. Also, err . . . send some fish to my house. The rest should be cooked for the evening function.'

The rest of the day was spent discussing the GOC's fishing abilities, with each officer outweighing the others' estimate in order to please the moody old man. His address to the jawans too was laced with fish innuendoes. So happy was the GOC with his angling skills that he referred to the enemy as a fish waiting to be trapped by the force of the mind.

Dinner was carefully planned by Sehmat, keeping in view the GOC's morning success at the lake. Everything possible was made to resemble a fish. Fishing nets were hung around the buffet tables with fish hooks, showcasing Thermocol replicas and cut-outs of the morning's catch. Sehmat even gave new names to cocktails and carried the first drink to the GOC herself.

Dressed carefully and strategically for the occasion, she looked stunningly beautiful. The GOC could not take his eyes off her the entire evening. She had draped her exquisite body in black crepe. The subtle lines of her long flowing gown accentuated her curves and the neckline, and though demurely cut, it was sensational.

He stood up as Sehmat approached him with a bearer and accepted the drink, looking closely at the colourful cocktail presented to him by such a lethally beautiful woman. On the brim of the glass sat a tiny fisherman resting under the shade of a paper umbrella. A small piece of pineapple, cut in the shape of a tiny fish, hung at the edge of the hook.

'It's your day, General. All the fish, it seems, fought amongst themselves to grab your hook. With so much catch, we did not feel the need to buy more from the market. Wish you many more,' Sehmat said and raised a toast, her sensual and mesmerizing eyes doing the talking, watching the hapless General fall into the trap.

Amir Khan took a large sip and rolled his tongue over his lips, tasting the liquor and simultaneously gulping down Sehmat's well-rehearsed compliment. 'You look very beautiful. Thank you very much for such magnificent arrangements. Yes indeed, what a day. Never in my life have I been so successful. I still can't believe my luck. And now you bring me this artistically designed cocktail. I hope there's no fish inside?'

'Oh! Nothing fishy, General. It's called the GOC Special.' And with that Sehmat walked away, diplomatically averting what could have been a faux pas.

Amir decided to take a walk around the huge lawns, admiring and repeatedly complimenting Sehmat on each detail. Everywhere he glanced, he noted and acknowledged the effort put in by the Sayeeds to make it a memorable night. Walking closely by his side, Sehmat ensured that the GOC saw the fishing hooks that were used as buttons on the flowing knee-length coats of the waiters.

'It was all Iqbal's idea, General. He felt that he might not be able to match you in fishing, but would surely outnumber the morning catch by the hooks on display tonight,' Sehmat gushed.

'So it was the Captain teaming up with his wife? I should have guessed. Well, let me admit, Begum Sahiba, how deeply I am touched by this most heartfelt warm welcome. Your family must be suitably rewarded for all the hard work. And I'll ensure that it happens sooner rather than later. Where's Iqbal posted now?'

'He is with the Light Infantry, base camp. Perhaps he could justify the power of his thinking if he could work with his GOC.'

Sehmat knew that most officers dreaded working under Amir Khan. But she was also aware of the many layers of officials who would act as a safe buffer for an officer of Iqbal's rank. Besides, she needed her own source at the GOC Headquarters.

The GOC too was aware of his own reputation and was taken aback by Sehmat's comments.

'I think you are right. There is indeed a shortage of thinkers in my office. Perhaps that will also ensure that we'll have the pleasure of your company more often, Begum Sahiba?'

'It indeed would entirely be my honour, General.'

'Good. Then let Iqbal join from next Monday. I'll issue the orders tomorrow. He can come in place of Major Hussein who's going for an advanced course.'

Iqbal was watching nervously from a distance. The ease with which his wife was handling the entire situation was making him sweat even more. The moment arrived when Sehmat subtly gestured to him to come and join her and the GOC. After standing momentarily at attention, he greeted the GOC. He prayed that his shaky legs would not give his nervousness away as he stood in front of the man who was infamous for his erratic behaviour.

Before the GOC could say anything, Sehmat reached out and excitedly grabbed her husband's hand. 'The GOC is impressed with your performance and has decided to promote you. You will now work under him in place of Major Hussein.'

Both the GOC and Iqbal were taken aback by Sehmat's comments. Noticing the change in their expressions, she inquired in a voice dripping with innocence, 'Did I say something wrong?'

Amir Khan quickly came to her rescue. 'Well not exactly a promotion, Iqbal, but you can perhaps be appointed as an acting Major since you would be replacing an officer of that rank.'

'Oh, thank you, Sir. I'll do my best to live up to your expectations,' Iqbal said and quickly came to a brief attention posture, his shoes clicking at the heels, acknowledging the good news. The GOC shook hands with him and looked over his shoulders at the approaching group of officers. Even without the extra perks and higher pay, Iqbal knew that he would be able to wear the rank and be eligible for a promotion. He looked at his wife in awe, knowing that he owed it to her. Through sheer planning and meticulous execution, she had brought him on a par with his elder brother.

Now on cloud nine, he headed towards the bar and ordered himself a rum and coke. He took a large sip and noticed a small plastic fish neatly hooked below the wedge of lime peacefully floating inside his glass. He quickly gulped his drink and pulled out the blue plastic. Finely etched under the belly of the fish was the three-letter word, GOC.

9

Two years passed. While Iqbal grew from strength to strength, he also became completely dependent on Sehmat for his day-to-day functioning. The father-in-law too found Sehmat indispensable and earned many brownie points from divisional headquarters by sharing operational details with his daughter-in-law.

In order to be appreciated amongst the socially relevant, the crème de la crème of the Pakistani society, Sehmat convinced her family to let her teach music in a reputed school. 'This would keep me productively busy,' she stressed. Since taking up jobs by women from high-profile families was not considered very dignified, Brigadier Sayeed took time to relent, but gave in after his son started lobbying for his wife.

Sehmat took time to shortlist the schools suited for her. She realized that there wasn't much choice when it came to providing quality education in music to children in upmarket schools. She settled for one that had the right mix of students from both rich and powerful families. Getting a job was not difficult as music teachers were not easy to come by. The principal was only too happy to accommodate her. Sehmat went through the records of past music teachers and was surprised to observe that no one had lasted for more than six months at a single stretch. She was determined to be different.

The following week, Sehmat found herself standing in front of a bunch of pupils belonging to the high and mighty, who had opted for music only because their parents wanted them to. When she entered the classroom, accompanied by the school administrator, she noticed that instead of rehearsing, the students were busy fighting over chocolates. Seeing a new teacher amidst them, the children stopped briefly but soon resumed their squabble without even acknowledging her presence. Sehmat hesitated but then reached for the big bowl of chocolates and pulled it away. There was firmness in her action, forcing the rich brats to retract. She placed the bowl gently on the shelf, turned towards them and without even introducing herself, began addressing them.

'Music comes from deep within. It opens the walls of the mind and helps in removing mental blocks. It's a great stepping stone to inner peace. It can help you attain name and fame and make your parents and country proud of you. If you want to be sincere about your goals, you will first have to lift yourself from small attachments and greed. Only then will you realize the innate strength of music.'

The class was stunned into silence. These students belonged to the most affluent part of society. More importantly, they knew the strength of their influence and many were not averse to using it to their advantage. The administrator too was stunned. He was an old hand and knew his limitations well as also the fact that no one had survived in the school by being strict with the students.

She added, 'Anybody can play the violin but only those succeed who free their minds from the greed of the surrounding materialistic world.'

Having made a lasting impression, she left the classroom for the day. The students remained in deep silence, pondering over the strong message. While locking the doors at the end of the day, the peon was amazed to find the half-filled chocolate bowl. He looked around, his face filled with surprise and disbelief, before stuffing his pockets with the booty.

Sehmat carefully scanned the list of her students as well as their kith and kin over the next week. She was good with children and knew that they had fragile egos. Her soft, mellow voice and tender mannerisms were in stark contrast to the previous music teacher who was mostly disliked. She shortlisted a young boy, Anwar Khan, to be groomed as the leader of the group. Much younger than most students, Anwar neither possessed natural talents nor had the ability to pick up the finer aspects of music.

Sehmat also realized that she would have to put in extra effort to bring Anwar up to even basic standards. But she had made up her mind to travel the extra mile. For all his drawbacks, Anwar had one strong credential: he was the grandson of the Pakistani army's second in command, Lieutenant General Imtiaz Khan.

As the annual day function came close, Sehmat helped Anwar to draw and paint an invitation for his grandfather. She then handed it over to Brigadier Sayeed and asked him to personally deliver it to the General in Islamabad.

'Give it to him in front of as many people as possible and explain to him the importance of his only grandson playing live to a large audience. Tell him that his presence will boost his grandson's morale.' Sehmat's voice was soft, but her confidence was now at its peak. She knew what she was saying. And, more importantly, the Brigadier too acknowledged her authority on the subject.

Brigadier Sayeed did as he was told and flew back with the General in an army aircraft well in time for the function. Sehmat and her students presented a memorable show that mesmerized the crowd. Sehmat stood facing her students, partially hidden by the huge stage curtain, softly murmuring the song being played on a dozen violins in unison. She knew the words by heart for she had sung them hundreds of times after coming to Pakistan.

> Oh winds please carry a message to my beloved country,
> Tell her that I am lonely without her,
> That I miss her and wish to be with her,
> Tell her that my life is nothing without her,
> And one day I shall return,
> To sleep peacefully in her lap forever,
> forever, forever, forever.

For Sehmat, the lyrics of the song struck a poignant chord. Though it was the children of Pakistan singing the song, her thoughts flew to her beloved country, its beautiful valleys, snow-peaked mountains, its fields of lush green meadows and the colours of its festivities. Her strong love for her parents and Aby, and the pain of losing him, was woven into this rich tapestry of memories. Despite her attempts to control her feelings, tears coursed down her cheeks unchecked.

Anwar became the centre of attention as the star performer of the show. The sombre notes of the violins as well as the deep timbre of the drum reached a feverish pitch and so did the young Anwar Khan's hands. On a cue, he turned towards the audience and stretched his hands sideways, bringing the show to an abrupt halt. There was a momentary hush in the hall. Then suddenly, as if to fill in the silence, the crowd began to clap. General Imtiaz Khan and his wife were astounded by what they had just heard. They knew their grandson did not have an ear for music and yet here he was. For them, Sehmat had brought about nothing short of a miracle, making their grandson and them the cynosure of all eyes.

Sehmat's young artistes graciously acknowledged the deafening applause and the standing ovation by the packed hall. The students stood in formation and bowed low while accepting the appreciation. They then turned towards the right-hand side of the stage where Sehmat stood, and knelt before her, urging her to come out. Sehmat was nonplussed and felt compelled to step out from behind the huge curtain. Despite her best efforts, she could not hide her tears, now flowing freely from her eyes. She stepped forward and hugged the students, simultaneously giving vent to her pent-up emotions.

The display of such dedication by a teacher towards her students deeply touched the audience, urging them to now give her a standing ovation. General Imtiaz Khan, who also doubled as the chief guest, was so impressed by the proceedings that he announced rewards for the school and also hosted a special dinner in Sehmat's honour. Little did he know that he was opening the doors of greater opportunity for the young Sehmat Khan.

While going to bed that night, Sehmat switched on the bedside light, pulled out her diary and began to scribble. She appeared immensely satisfied with the day's progress, but, deep inside, her heart ached. Half an hour later, she read aloud the couplets of her poem in a controlled and soft voice. Her verses floated freely in the closed confines of the room, carrying traces of her pain.

Oh Nature

Caged in the wrap of time,
Surrounded by lust and desire,
Holding on to greed for more,
A bird within me wishes to fly free.

Far away from shores,
In the middle of nowhere,
Am rowing my life's boat in materialistic circles,
Wondering how to free my soul,
Hoping yet to fly free.

I miss the shine of sun,
The song of birds,
The clouds hugging the winds,
The purity of dewdrops and love,
I desire yet to quench my thirst,
I yet aim to fly free.

I have emotions that are meaningless,
Courage that is worthless,

I have a journey ahead that is aimless,
I dream yet to reach my destination,
I yet pray to fly free.

In a jungle of steel, mud and concrete,
Packed with scores like me as sardines,
Tied in knots of social bonds,
And hopeless hopes,
I see my shadow amidst millions,
I do not learn yet and change,
I still yearn to fly free.

Oh nature, dear nature, are you listening?

As the last lines of her poem merged with the stillness of the
night, she put the diary aside, closed her eyes and sank into
the soft plush pillow.

Iqbal, who lay asleep on the left side of the bed, woke
up as the lights went off. He could not make much of the
poem, but the pain in her voice was evident to him. He could
neither fathom the depth of her poetry, nor muster sufficient
courage to ask her. With deep furrows between his brows, he
struggled hard to find a meaning to it, before falling asleep.

* * *

It did not take long for Sehmat to learn that General Imtiaz
Khan was also a golf aficionado. She missed no opportunity
to build bridges with the rest of his clan and began following
the game closely. In less than three weeks, she succeeded in

fixing a game of golf for Brigadier Sayeed and simultaneously made a plan to get her father-in-law promoted. The next fortnight was spent in training a small dog to run away with the golf ball.

Sehmat studied the game at great length and pored over volumes of books, learning the subtleties and nuances of the elite sport. And the more she read, the more fascinated she became. 'Golfers' psyche is completely different,' she read. 'They are a breed apart. It is common for a golfer to postpone an important issue, overlook a commitment or even forget his wife's birthday or their wedding anniversary. But it is unlikely for a golfer to forget his victories on the golf course. He cherishes each win, however friendly the match play, and even decades later does not miss recalling its minutest detail over a drink.' She was further shocked to learn of terms like 'golfing widows' and how a true golfer would prefer to be on the golf course than in bed with his wife.

Armed with adequate knowledge, Sehmat scheduled Sayeed's game during a routine visit to the Army Chief's house. She also included two serving judges as part of the four-ball. She strategically shortlisted the judges in order to give an upper hand to the General after taking into account his shortcomings and strengths. Sayeed became General Khan's natural partner, and the friendly four-ball game became an unofficial match play between the army and judiciary.

This was also an opportunity for Sehmat to get closer to Abdul. She asked her father-in-law to involve their most faithful servant in the game plan.

'Who can be better trusted than Abdul Mian for this vital task, Abba Huzoor?' she forcefully reiterated in the presence of Abdul but without disclosing the nature of the work. The genuineness in her tone and respect in her voice was not missed by Abdul either. His face was writ with elements of surprise. His questioning eyes focused on the Brigadier, searching for an answer. But Sayeed remained silent and merely smiled in return.

She then left the two men to themselves and went inside the haveli. Minutes later, the two old men were talking to each other in confidence. Abdul's head went up and down at constant intervals, nodding and acknowledging the commands from his master. He didn't quite understand the nuances of the game but interacted with Sehmat extensively over the next week in order to master his own part. Sehmat's plan to soften Abdul's stance towards her was coming to fruition.

Sehmat blocked the course for the first hour of play citing security concerns. It also helped her restrict the movement of the spectators. As they teed off, the first four holes matched evenly, with the judges displaying exceptional play to keep the army team in check.

The fifth tee off was a par-three hole. It was also hidden partially by trees and a hillock. The golfers could just about see the flag on the green before shooting the ball in the air. Sehmat had cleverly placed the same brand of ball in the hole before the start of the game and let Sayeed's trusted servant, Abdul, take charge of the canine.

Imtiaz Khan was a keen player, but like most golfers, had never hit a hole-in-one. On the fifth hole, as the General swung the club, Brigadier Sayeed and the judges clapped in unison, acknowledging the fine hit. The ball went high in the air, heading towards the green. All eyes were focused on the flight path, and it was important for Sehmat to divert their attention from Abdul to let the dog complete the drill.

Sensing opportunity, Sehmat faked her own fall while attempting to balance herself on the uneven ground. The General leaped forward to lend a helping hand, quickly followed by the rest of the party who fussed over her, inquiring if she had hurt herself. The diversion gave ample time for the trained canine to run on the green and vanish into the arms of the partially hidden Abdul, with the white ball firmly lodged in his mouth.

The General reached the green and looked for his ball, while Sayeed casually walked towards the hole. His heart was beating fast. He knew from Sehmat's expressions that the plan had been pulled through successfully. But he also realized that one mistake could mean curtains for his career. Brigadier Sayeed pretended to look here and there before walking up to the hole. He peeped in and lifted the flag by its steel shaft, exclaiming with joy.

'It's in the hole, Sir,' Sayeed's excitement now reached a feverish pitch, leaving the bewildered Chief dumbstruck. He had been playing golf for decades without coming anywhere close to the hole in his first shot. And here he was, holding the ball that was soon to become part of a glittering hole-in-one trophy.

The game was called off. The grand party that followed was dedicated to Sehmat, since it was at her insistence that the General had agreed to play, in turn fulfilling his lifetime ambition of achieving this feat. That it was achieved in the company of two high court judges lent further credibility to his achievement.

'You have been a good omen for both my grandson as well as for me, Begum Sahiba,' Imtiaz Khan said. 'We are grateful to you for bringing so much happiness to all of us. I wonder if I'll ever get an opportunity to reciprocate the favour.' Sehmat simply nodded and instead of accepting the credit, thanked Allah for his grace. The General and his wife felt deeply touched by Sehmat's humility. Mrs Khan went a step further and offered her any assistance that she might need in the future and also gave her personal contact number. For the young Anwar Khan, his teacher became his godmother and raison d'être for his growing confidence levels.

Within two weeks, Sayeed was promoted to the rank of Major General and given the coveted post of Deputy Chief of the Inter-Services Intelligence or ISI. While Major Mehboob had ample reasons to sulk, feeling ignored and sidelined by his own father, Sehmat soon began to look into the top-secret assets of the Pakistani army.

Even though she grew in stature at the Sayeed household, Sehmat foresaw her brother-in-law's plight. Consequently, she did everything possible to get closer to the Munira–Mehboob duo. She accompanied Munira for shopping, took her advice in running the daily chores at the haveli and presented her with exclusive perfumes, clothes and gifts. Major Mehboob became fond of her too and appreciated Sehmat's commitment towards the family. He was impressed with the fact that Sehmat gave importance to his wife and did not put her down.

For some reason, however, Abdul still could not bring himself to trust the youngest daughter-in-law and continued to keep a watch on her. His attitude towards her did soften but he did not let down his guard. Abdul took any suggestion made by Sehmat with a pinch of salt. He was a simple human being and so was his thought process. So much so that Sehmat could practically see through him. Sehmat could not build bridges with him and had to remain content with the fact that he had begun to restrain himself from talking ill of her behind her back. Sehmat was also aware of Abdul's prying eyes that kept a close check on her movements. She was not perturbed since she enjoyed the complete confidence of the entire family.

Instinctively, however, she kept reminding herself that she was far from safe.

10

Back in Delhi, Mir found himself astounded by the zeal and enthusiasm with which cryptic messages were being transmitted at regular intervals by Hidayat's daughter. She was working under her own steam, needing no motivation. He was deeply touched by the ease with which she had made the sacrifice. It must not have been easy to walk away from the man she loved, especially when she had the choice to do otherwise. Living in an alien country, which was turning into an arch-enemy with every passing day, would have made life even more difficult. He often wondered if Sehmat was purging her guilt by giving her all for the country. But his bigger concern was the undue risk she was beginning to take in transmitting signals. She had to be told to go slow before she got into serious trouble.

Sehmat's assignment took over her very being. Following her father's footsteps, her duty towards her nation became her first religion. She would often spend the entire night plotting, scheming, strategizing and trying to find ways and avenues to secure vital information. Her days were spent making new contacts and charming acquaintances just in case they could provide her with something significant. She never once forgot the fact that she was from the enemy country and forgave those who were wary of her.

One evening, as Sehmat was routinely searching through her father-in-law's top-secret files, she saw something that pulled the ground from under her feet. So vital was the information that she dared not make an error. The information suggested that Pakistani submarines were preparing to set sail for the Indian coast. With trembling hands, she held the document, her apprehension rising with every word she scanned. 'Keep Vikrant within striking range,' was the brief order. The file also contained a photograph of INS Vikrant, India's only aircraft carrier, and gave details of the weaponry and manpower it carried on board.

Realizing the magnitude and significance of the information, she took the folder to her bathroom. She did not want to miss out on any data she intended to transmit. The file contained complex area coordinates of where the submarines were to be initially stationed. With her heart beating wildly, she was in the process of signalling the vital information by Morse code directly to Mir, when Abdul knocked on the door. Her father-in-law had come home early and was desperately looking for the same file. Sehmat was not surprised.

The entire household was empty even though it was evening. Her sister-in-law was at her parents' home. Her husband, brother-in-law and father-in-law had been extremely occupied for the past two weeks, returning home late in the night. The Pakistani army was secretly preparing for an impending attack on India. And unlike previous wars that were fought only by the army on both sides, this time Pakistan was pushing its navy and the air force into the battle.

Sehmat had never seen a submarine in her life and wasn't even aware of how it looked, but from the classified documents, she could make out that these were special vessels that could sail under water and remain undetected beneath the sea for weeks together. Appreciating the gravity of the file, she tried to grasp as much knowledge as she possibly could. But Abdul's persistent knocks on her door and inquiries about the missing folder were making it difficult for Sehmat to complete the job.

She finally responded and directed him to wait for her in the living room. Her tone was curt and voice crisp enough to cause humiliation. Sehmat realized that she was left with no choice but to put the servant in his place if she had to complete the job at hand. Abdul retreated slowly, his face clouded with deep anguish and hurt. No one in the family had spoken to him in such a harsh tone in many decades. His head dropped as he turned slowly towards the living room.

Hurriedly, Sehmat transmitted the rest of the message and placed the document back in the manila envelope. She concealed the packet inside her shawl and made for Sayeed's study. However, in her haste, she did not dismantle the transmission keys inside the bathroom. But she locked her bedroom door before rushing to the anxious old man. Her face was remarkably calm, masking her inner turmoil and nervousness.

She deliberately entered through the rear end of the study and placed the envelope amongst the numerous files. Then, briskly manoeuvring through bookshelves, she reached the other end of the room to face her father-in-law. On seeing her, his face lit up, and he described to her the purpose of his early return—he was looking for a file. Tactfully, Sehmat moved him to his room and advised him to relax while she went about the search. She was back in five minutes, holding in her hand the lost envelope. Sayeed took a quick glance inside the yellow cover to satisfy himself with the contents, thanked Sehmat profusely for the timely help and rushed into the waiting flag car.

After seeing him off, Sehmat went back to her room. To her horror, she found both the bedroom and bathroom doors ajar. With a sick feeling in the pit of her stomach, she noticed that the Morse code key machine had been uprooted and removed from its base plate. She rushed out and saw a familiar shadow moving through the kitchen towards the rear lawns. Sehmat stood at the door in a daze for a while, watching the shadow vanish into the darkness. She looked around. An army ration supply truck on a routine visit was parked near the rear entrance of the haveli. That was all she needed to carry out her impromptu plan. Barefooted, and not even bothering to put on slippers, she quickly stepped into the military vehicle.

She glanced over her shoulder to make sure she was not being watched by any of the servants. She then hastily jumped into the driver's seat, placed an old hat lying on top of the steering wheel on her head and pushed the ignition switch with all her strength, praying that it wouldn't let her down. She had just one aim—to eliminate the only witness to her act of espionage. With a shuddering loud noise, the three-ton vehicle roared into action and began rolling towards the main road. For the first fifty metres the truck moved in a zigzag pattern but soon settled into a straight line, without causing undue suspicion.

She steadied the heavy machine with her frail hands and drove in the same direction in which Abdul had set off, till she reached the barrier checkpoint. A lone sentry sitting near the temporary hut stood up, anticipating that the truck would stop for the mandatory check. It was reasonably dark by then but Sehmat's face was lit with firm determination. Under no circumstances was she going to let her mission fail. Pressing the gas pedal, she pushed the engine to full throttle and drove past the checkpost, ploughing through the barrier. The sentry jumped backwards in a hurry, hurling the choicest abuses.

At the T-junction, Sehmat turned towards Major Mehboob's office which was situated nearest to the haveli. Given Abdul's closeness to Mehboob, Sehmat knew he would not seek refuge anywhere else. She felt that he would not pass this damning information and equipment to any outsider, and in turn put the Sayeeds' reputation at risk and ridicule.

The vehicle was gaining speed and it was becoming difficult for the petite and delicate Sehmat to control it, but she remained seated in the driver's seat, her eyes focused on the road ahead. The truck rumbled on for another hundred metres before slowing down considerably. Not too far ahead, in the centre of the road, was Abdul, running as fast as his aged legs could carry him.

On hearing the sound of the approaching truck, he stopped briefly to check its identity. His normally cold eyes visibly lit up noticing the army vehicle. He gasped for breath and started waving frantically with both hands, screaming 'stop, stop' at the same time. He was wearing army overalls that Major Mehboob had given him not too long ago.

The truck slowed further as it neared Abdul. Sehmat's steely hands gripped the wheel and her brilliant-blue eyes shone, looking at the vulnerable servant like a jungle cat looks at its hapless prey. Momentarily though, she felt weak in her knees. Her entire body shook with anticipation and her blood ran cold at the thought of what she was about to do. Her forehead was bathed in sweat, which she wiped with the back of her hand with a gesture of impatience.

She had always admired Abdul for his blind loyalty and commitment towards her in-laws. But she was left with little choice. If only Abdul had stuck to his duties as a servant and not sneaked around, she would not have been forced to take such a barbaric step. Her eyes were moist, but she knew she would have to destroy the evidence together with the witness if she was to serve her country for more time.

'I am sorry, Abdul, but you have to go. My country comes first,' she murmured before pressing her right foot on the gas pedal.

Abdul's face was aghast with horror. Perhaps he had recognized Sehmat's face hidden beneath the old khaki hat. The crunch of the old man's body being crushed by the heavy truck made Sehmat want to get out and retch. The sickening sound would stay with her and torture her for the rest of her life.

She drove the truck for another kilometre or so before turning it sharply into a narrow lane. Bringing the heavy metallic mass of destruction to an abrupt halt, she jumped out and rushed across the service lane into a row of badly lit quarters belonging to the junior staff—mainly helpers and servants of the army officers.

Using the eerie darkness to her advantage, Sehmat walked briskly past a few blocks. She spotted a burka hanging on a clothes line and quickly slipped it on. It literally covered her from head to toe. She resumed her long and tense walk towards the cantonment and refused to let her mind be swayed by what she had done.

She had memorized every detail of the area and was familiar with the lanes, byways and shortcuts that would help her reach the haveli quickly. Protected by her black veil, she moved stealthily, a dark figure in the even darker moonless night. But to Sehmat, it felt like trying to walk away from the unpardonable sin she had just committed.

After what seemed an eternity, she reached the haveli. She approached the sprawling mansion from its back entry and sneaked towards the kitchen door. She then picked up a stone and broke open a small tile on the side of the first step at the rear entrance. Wrapped in a plastic sheet was a metallic key neatly stuck under the broken tile. Sehmat had planted the key within a week of her arrival at her in-laws, in anticipation of such an exigency. Mir had repeatedly stressed the importance of arranging an exit route before she undertook the mission.

Opening the gate noiselessly, she surveyed her surroundings. Thankfully no one was home yet, and she ran through the rear lawns past the kitchen till she stumbled into the safety of her room. Locking herself in the bathroom, she took deep breaths and gasped for air. Her hair was a mess and so was she. Someone only had to see her face to figure that there was something fishy about her. She splashed water on her face, undressed in a hurry and then walked into the dimly lit room, leaving the bathroom door ajar. Using the bathroom light, she sat at the edge of the fireplace and lit it with shaking hands. She then went back into the bathroom and turned on the water taps. Sinking into the bathtub, she scrubbed herself, cleansing the evening's incident off her mind. But she failed to wash off the guilt of the murder, the cold-bloodedness with which she had taken the life of an old man.

The heavy burden on her conscience began to press upon her and she began crying even as she towelled herself dry. Fifteen minutes later, Sehmat stepped out of the bathroom. She used the same burka to wipe both the passage and her room, removing visible traces of mud and evidence that could incriminate her. Minutes later she was back in the bathroom, dismantling the communication lines and loosely hanging wires. Bundling the burka and the house gown, she threw them in the fire pit without ceremony and sat next to it till the evidence was completely consumed by the hungry flames. Her feet were aching and fatigue was beginning to take over her whole body.

Her mind raced back over the entire episode from the moment she'd rushed to meet her father-in-law. If only she had been more careful, she wouldn't have had to destroy a life. Returning to the scene of the murder, she visualized the chronological order of Abdul's last moments. She had hit Abdul head-on, crushing him under the wheels. She was sure he'd died instantaneously. She wasn't bothered about the truck either, it would have been found by now.

Drinking was a common practice amongst army drivers. The truck's presence near the drivers' quarters would make the overworked, underpaid babus dismiss the case as one of drunken driving. But she still had a nagging doubt about Abdul. She had no means of finding out his status and had to wait like a sitting duck for daybreak.

The only bright spot in the entire gamut of things was that she had fulfilled her duty and had transmitted some extremely vital information. Her father would have been proud of her work, though she was not sure if her act of damage control was sufficient to keep her head afloat.

11

For the hundredth time, Mir read the note: Pakiz moving troops to Chumb. War inevitable. Subs setting sail to east coast. Attack on aircraft carrier imminent. Monitor following coordinates.

The implications were serious. He stroked his jaw in deep concentration as he carefully considered and analysed the dead reckoning (DR) positions where the subs were to be positioned. Transferring the positions on the chart, he encircled the areas and stepped back to take a macro view.

As per Sehmat's information, Pakistani submarines were being stationed not only in the Arabian Sea that surrounded the heavily guarded Western Command of the Indian Navy, but also in the Bay of Bengal that housed warships under the Eastern Naval Command. The more he analysed the report, the more clear it became to Mir that Pakistan was bent upon confrontation. Reports of support from the American fleet, present in the vicinity of the Arabian Sea had possibly skyrocketed the Pakistani government's morale.

Mir's office was keeping a close watch on the rapidly rising graph of red pointers on the map. With each passing day, more Pakistani troops moved closer to the Indian border, with battle tanks and armoury, indicating the impending Pakistani attack. However, experts and war analysts on the Indian side remained divided on whether such a gathering of troops would lead to a full-fledged Indo-Pak war. 'Pakistan does not have the wherewithal,' they strongly felt. 'Pakistan cannot open war on two fronts and survive,' they repeatedly opined. And the analysts did have strong reasons in support of their arguments.

At that time, Pakistan was heavily engaged with its trouble-torn eastern state where the public at large had come out in revolt against the step-motherly treatment it had received at the hands of its rulers. To curb the uprising, the Pakistani government had stationed huge army contingents and paramilitary forces under a Lieutenant General at Dhaka. Logistically however, it was a nightmare for the state, separated by the huge land mass of India on one side and an even bigger seafront on the other, to govern effectively. Poor communication systems, unmanageable expenditures and prolonged delays in providing logistical support to its massive contingent were enormous challenges in themselves.

Taking on a much larger country like India and at the same time militarily curbing the uprising in its own state located far away from mainland Pakistan logically appeared nothing short of suicidal. A seaward-bound submarine attack on Indian shores was even more difficult to fathom for the Indian think tank. Besides, climatically, winter was not best suited for war as the prevailing low temperatures in the northern region could cause untold miseries. The intelligence reports were thus viewed with suspicion and not taken at face value.

Despite their strong logic, Mir wasn't convinced. Sehmat's information, based on her first-hand knowledge, was too precise and accurate to be ignored. It was safer to assume that Pakistan was likely to engage India in the thickest of winters, much against past convention. The counter-view analysts argued that the Pakistani forces could utilize the surprise element and inflict maximum damage in quick succession before seeking the help of Western countries to enforce ceasefire. And there could be no bigger damage to the Indian pride than the sinking of its flagship, the mighty British-built aircraft carrier, INS Vikrant.

Pakistan was displaying its will to go to any extent to achieve its aim by sailing Ghazi, Hangor and Mangro into Indian waters even as it was engaged in a dialogue with the country. As if propelled by a sudden brainwave, Mir rushed to the Navy Chief. He looked like someone who had just solved a jigsaw puzzle. And it was all because of one daredevil woman, Sehmat.

'I would give due weightage to the information and position Vikrant out of harm's way, maybe over here, till we are fully assured of her safety,' Mir said, picking up a small model of INS Vikrant, and placing it at the Cochin harbour which was well protected from the possible sub attacks. He then turned towards the Admiral with raised eyebrows, expecting to be commended for his valuable contribution.

It was now the Navy Chief's turn to get in on the act. After all, the Indian intelligence services were not supposed to decide where and how the naval fleet would move. Analysing the enemy submarine positions on the chart, the Admiral lifted the model from its position at the Cochin harbour and positioned it at the Andaman harbour. His face displayed tension, unhappiness and wrinkles of dissatisfaction. 'I hope your intelligence report is correct, Mir. The carrier has some boiler problems. This move will practically put her out of a job.'

'The information is correct, Admiral,' replied Mir almost immediately. 'We are lucky to be forewarned, for these subs are not easy to detect.' Mir's mind was racing in all directions, his thoughts invariably hovering around Sehmat's safety. He was almost certain that Sehmat was in grave danger. She couldn't have transmitted such a long message so accurately without it getting picked up by enemy receivers as well. Plus her 'do or die' attitude over the past few days had further added to his fears. Excusing himself, he left the war room and rushed to his office. He tried to reach the Indian Embassy in Pakistan, but each time the call got disconnected. 'Bastards!' he spat aloud and pressed the intercom button as hard as he could with his right thumb.

Startled, Javed, his assistant, came running in. 'Call the Indian Embassy. Tell the High Commissioner that I am reaching Islamabad by the first flight tomorrow.'

'Yes, Sir,' Javed replied and took the receiver from Mir's hand, replacing it on the cradle. It was rare to see his boss, who always maintained his composure during trying circumstances, so shaken up. Without uttering a word, he left the room. Moments later, Javed was busy cancelling Mir's appointments for the rest of the day, including the dinner that his boss was hosting for his daughter's in-laws.

Back in the briefing room, the Navy Chief was huddled with the other Admirals, brainstorming on the numerous probabilities and options. In comparison to the army, theirs was a younger and more inexperienced force that had never been put to the test. The lone aircraft carrier, INS Vikrant, was one of their main weapons, capable of launching air attacks from the middle of the ocean. But it was also vulnerable to submarine attack and thus needed to be protected first. Any damage to the floating airstrip could not only result in the loss of thousands of men on board, it could also demoralize and severely embarrass the armed forces. For Pakistan, on the other hand, Vikrant was the coveted trophy they aspired to acquire. Having faced defeat in every showdown in the past, its desperate Generals were pushing hard to level scores at any cost.

12

Major Mehboob stood helplessly by Abdul's bedside at the military hospital. Blood oozed from his head and most parts of his wrecked body. His breathing was slow and laboured. The doctors attending to him had given up hope and said as much to Major Mehboob when he had rushed in, demanding to be allowed a visit.

'It's a miracle that he has survived this long but I am afraid there's no hope. It's a matter of a few minutes in fact. Same old story of drunken driving by these reckless jawans, I am afraid. We ought to do something serious about it. The only word he uttered repeatedly was your name. It took us a while to figure it out and link it to you. It seems as if he wants to tell you something,' the surgeon said helplessly. Leaving Abdul in Major Mehboob's custody, the doctor exited the room, lamenting the growing lawlessness.

'Thanks, Colonel,' Major Mehboob said to the departing doctor as he bent over Abdul, surprised to see the faithful servant staring hard at him. Abdul's eyes were strangely gripped with fear, his lips on the verge of saying something. Then he tried to move, and from under the blanket, he managed to pull out his right hand. It was covered with thick, dried blood. He painstakingly opened his tightly held fist. His broken fingers made crackling noises as he did so, exposing two small metal pieces. He emptied them on to his master's hand.

Mehboob gingerly took the scraps in his hands, trying to fathom what the dying man was saying. 'Yes, Abdul, what is it? Tell me?' he said gently.

Abdul tried as hard as he could, gathering every ounce of strength. His lips moved rapidly but no sound came out of them. His head had suffered the maximum damage. Mehboob bent down to bring his ear next to Abdul's lips, simultaneously encouraging him to speak.

Using all his energy, Abdul managed to murmur inaudibly, 'Hhh . . . hhh . . . mat, mat,' and then with an agonizing groan, gave in to the darkness of death.

Mehboob stared at the eyes that were still wide open and glued to his face, pleading him to solve the mystery. 'Abdul, Abdul! Wait! Tell me, please, Abdul!' Mehboob shook the lifeless form, urging him to come back to life and throw light on the baffling shreds of metal.

On hearing him shout, the doctor rushed in and pulled Mehboob away from the dead man. Balancing himself and shrugging the doctor away, Mehboob walked back to Abdul's side. He then gently placed his palm over his forehead and closed his accusing eyes.

The Major took off his cap and stood in silent respect for a while before walking back to his car. With the metal shards still clutched in his hand, Mehboob tried to make sense of what had just happened. What had Abdul wanted to convey?

Whatever it was, Mehboob knew it was vital. Abdul had tenaciously clung on to life, demanding to see him. There was something he wanted to say to Mehboob. Whatever Abdul wanted to say was serious and connected to the metal pieces that were now in his possession. But what was the old man trying to say? And where did the pieces of metal come from?

All through the journey, Mehboob kept looking at the bloodstained black pieces. He turned them around, pulled and pushed the tiny metallic rods and even tried to bend them. The more he attempted, the further he felt from solving the mystery. As the car halted at the haveli's portico, the driver jumped out and ran across to open the rear door, only to find the Major still deeply engrossed in examining the two pieces. 'Sir,' the driver said respectfully, breaking Mehboob's reverie.

Mehboob slammed the door of the car in frustration and walked past the prying eyes of servants and jawans. He appeared visibly disturbed. His head was splitting with the effort of deciphering Abdul's last message. There was no beginning or end. Abdul had died carrying a deep secret with him.

As soon as he entered the main hall, he summoned the servants and broke the news, keenly observing each face, to look for any suspicious reaction. Failing there too, he asked for Sehmat and briefed her about Abdul's death and the two metal pieces that he had mysteriously left behind.

Sehmat had trained herself not to show any signs of relief at the news of Abdul's death. Had the Major observed her closely, he would have noticed her lack of expression at the bad news, but he was too preoccupied to notice the beads of sweat that Sehmat cleverly wiped off using her forearm. Recovering quickly, she expressed shock and dismay, and feigned ignorance about the two pieces displayed on the table. However, it soon became clear to Sehmat that the Major was not going to rest till he unveiled the truth. 'Abdul has been murdered in cold blood,' he repeatedly told his wife, Munira, who too urged her husband to unravel the mystery. She had immediately returned to the haveli after hearing about Abdul's death. It now became clear to Sehmat that she would soon have to decide her brother-in-law's fate as well if she wanted to protect the operation.

Back in her room later, Sehmat sat heavily on her bed, feeling an enormous weight descend upon her. Killing Abdul was a necessity. But she had no way to find out if Mehboob really remembered Abdul's final words. She realized that she could not take any risks at such a crucial hour. Her brother-in-law would probably recall the servant's dying words once he got over the shock.

Pacing the floor of her room, Sehmat concluded that she had no choice. The incident had triggered a chain reaction. And to protect her country's fate, she would have to kill yet again. An hour later, she slipped into a burka and left for Jama Masjid, announcing that she wanted to offer prayers for the departed soul.

Using the most crowded entrance to the mosque, she slipped into the nearby phone booth and dialled a number. She stood at a vantage point from where she could see the road clearly. Once done, she returned to the cool interiors of the mosque and waited for a reasonable amount of time to pass. Half an hour later, she went back to the waiting car.

She was about to sit in the car when a woman's pleading voice made her turn around.

'Madam, please buy this umbrella. It is very good and you will find it very handy. I need the money to pay for food for my family.'

Sehmat's driver immediately rushed to her side. He blocked Sehmat from the woman and asked her to get inside the vehicle. Sehmat complied. He then closed the door and ran back to the driver's seat. He was about to start the car when he heard Sehmat talking to the same woman through the window.

'How much do you want for this umbrella?'

'So very kind of you, Madam. Please give me whatever you like.'

Sehmat pulled out two crisp hundred-rupee bills from her purse, handed the money to the woman and took the umbrella. The driver was about to advise Sehmat against paying such a large amount for something so useless, but stopped himself short. 'These rich people,' he thought to himself with disdain, and pressed the accelerator. Driving expertly through the crowded road, he looked at Sehmat's reflection in the rear-view mirror. Her face was pale and drawn, a picture of grief.

'You should not have given so much to her,' he rebuked her kindly. 'They are always begging around the mosque,' he said, his voice softening at the sight of her unhappy face.

'It is completely okay. I have helped a starving family in Abdul's name. May God grant peace to the departed soul,' Sehmat's voice was low and filled with emotion but rang like the chime of a cuckoo clock in the driver's ears for a long time. He was visibly moved by Sehmat's gesture and refrained from further conversation. Sehmat saw a look of approval cross the driver's face in the front mirror. She anticipated that word of her charity in Abdul's name would spread to everyone at the haveli. She wished that to happen because she needed every bit of support if she had to pull herself out of the current mess.

Back in her room, Sehmat locked the door and placed the umbrella on the bed. She then carefully studied the handle and located a tiny press-button. She unscrewed the handle gently and took out a cylindrical bottle wrapped in a small piece of handwritten paper. She read the note: 'By pressing this button, you can inject tiny drops of mercury into a human body. Though the process will not hurt, the mercury will act soon and within hours the person will suffer a heart attack.'

Sehmat tore the paper into tiny pieces and flushed it down the toilet. She waited till the bits of paper disappeared and then screwed the handle back to its original position. A faint click indicated that the mercury cylinder inside the handle was primed. She then placed the umbrella at the back of her closet and turned the key.

An hour later, the telephone rang with one short ring and disconnected. Springing into action, Sehmat positioned herself near the phone. When it rang again, she snatched it from its cradle and whispered breathlessly, 'Yes, go on. This is me.' For the next couple of minutes she listened intently to the caller. Then, without saying a word, she replaced the receiver. She went back to the closet, pulled out the umbrella and left in the same car, carrying an ordinary-looking handbag.

'Please take me to Main Bazaar. I would like to buy clothes for the poor so that Abba Huzoor can distribute them when he arrives tomorrow,' she directed the driver. The driver acknowledged with a nod of his head.

He shook his head sadly when they passed the broken barricade.

'Someone must have been absurdly drunk to have done this last night, Madam,' he began conversationally. Sehmat did not respond and the driver remained silent till they reached the market. Alighting from the rear seat, Sehmat directed him to take the car to the parking lot and wait for her return. She then headed for the market complex and disappeared into the ladies' toilet.

Minutes later, a woman clad in a black burka emerged. She was carrying an umbrella in her hand. Walking past the complex, the burka-clad woman hailed a taxi. Fifteen minutes later, she was walking briskly towards the office of 'Bureau of Inspections'. She looked at her watch before entering the compound. She climbed the stairs to the first floor and then waited for an agonizing twenty minutes near the open window. A car approached the building and stopped at the entrance. The door of the car flew open, letting an army officer clad in a dark-green uniform step out. He began climbing the portico stairs. Sehmat lifted her veil to watch him carefully for a few moments, satisfying herself of his identity. She then pulled the thin cloth back over her eyes and slowly began descending the stairs.

Major Mehboob was coming from the other end, climbing briskly. He had a brown paper packet in his right hand, the contents of which were known to Sehmat. She stopped a few yards away from him and pretended to struggle with the handle of her umbrella. When Major Mehboob reached where she stood, she tripped and deliberately fell on him. Being the gentleman he was, Mehboob held her by her arms and steadied her till she regained her balance.

'Hai Allah! I am sorry,' Sehmat said in a husky tone before stepping aside in mock embarrassment.

The Major simply smiled in acknowledgement of the stranger's apology and walked on. Sehmat turned to see if her little operation had been successful. The Major continued walking at the same pace, lightly rubbing his arm at the same time. He had no time to look at the tiny puncture wound there. In a matter of seconds, he had reached the end of the corridor. He did not look back, but Sehmat did and turned towards the building entrance to take one last glimpse of her brother-in-law.

She stood there for a while, looking at the receding figure of the tall young man. Tears coursed down her cheeks as she thought of his pretty wife and the tragedy that would soon befall the Sayeeds. 'I carry the price of your blood on my hands and in my soul, Mehboob Bhai. I wonder if I will be able to live with the guilt,' she said to the retreating figure. 'I am truly sorry, but I had to do this. My country comes first.'

Sehmat walked the better part of the distance and hailed a taxi back to the same market. Minutes later, she re-emerged from the same toilet but without the cover of the traditional burka. Instead, she now carried a large packet of clothes meant for distribution to the poor. The umbrella had been disposed of and every inch of the toilet wiped carefully, leaving no fingerprints. The remaining drops of mercury had been flushed down the toilet and the equipment discarded in two different garbage cans. Two hours later, she was sitting with her sister-in-law in the living room, discussing the growing incidences of drunken driving.

13

General Sayeed and Major Iqbal sat side by side, receiving the long stream of visitors who were arriving in large numbers. The compound was packed with politicians, bureaucrats, industrialists and army officers who had come to pay their last respects to Major Mehboob Sayeed. The General was visibly shaken and looked shattered. The doctors at the Military Hospital had attributed his death to a massive heart attack, but Munira linked it to the shock he had received due to the accidental death of their most faithful servant, Abdul.

General Sayeed was torn between his duty as a father and being the second in command of the ISI that was in the midst of finalizing a war on its neighbouring country. He could just about manage a short leave to attend the two funerals. Despite the double tragedy, he was constantly engaged on the phone, taking briefings and addressing crucial issues. Every part of his body wore the signs of stress and fatigue. He could not come to terms with the death of his elder son and that had kept him up the whole night. The sprightly General had aged.

While Major Iqbal handled the rites and formalities, General Sayeed shuffled between the drawing room, attending mostly to the VIPs, and his study, to be regularly updated with developments on the rapidly developing war theatre. Sehmat remained on the sidelines and attended to Major Mehboob's widow. The moment was ripe, and she knew that every scrap of information she could lay her hands on could prove vital. In his grief, the General had become careless and, on a few rare occasions, had even left classified files on his table, forgetting to lock them in his safe.

This was the moment Sehmat was waiting for. There was no Abdul to keep a watch on her. All the servants, family members and relatives were busy attending to the unending stream of mourners. Utilizing the opportunity, she repeatedly slipped into the General's study and sifted through the classified documents.

On the second day, an exhausted General Sayeed appeared to be on the verge of collapse. Seizing the moment, Sehmat offered to help him 'clear the clutter' on his desk and pack his briefcase before he left for an important meeting the next morning. The General, emotionally drained and too tired to refuse, readily accepted her offer.

Sehmat assisted him in sealing two secret envelopes that were to be sent to the Prime Minister of Pakistan, but not before going through their contents. Both letters contained information on the Indian preparedness, political developments and military status. The papers also contained details of secret agents based in New Delhi who were providing vital information to the ISI and needed to be shifted to safety.

This time around, Sehmat had to think of a better, more foolproof plan to transfer her information to the right ears. She was experienced enough to value the information she had just acquired, and also aware that all telephone lines to the Indian consulate would be tapped. Any communication therefore could prove fatal. Yet she had to find an alternative. She was disturbed by this predicament, but the gloom in the house was such that she did not look different from the others. She kept brainstorming till she came up with a solution.

The funeral procession was long, but the motorcade moved quickly to the burial ground where both the bodies were laid to rest side by side. After the prayers, as the visitors departed, Iqbal removed name slips from the wreaths in order to send 'thank you' notes later. Meanwhile, Sehmat escorted Mehboob's widow to the waiting car and helped her sit on the rear seat. Her mind was more focused on the newly acquired information than on providing moral support to Munira. She sat adjacent to Munira, waited for her to settle down and then said, 'Can we go to a nearby mosque and offer prayers before going home?' Sehmat's eyes were focused on Munira, hoping for a positive response.

Instead Munira said, 'No, Sehmat, I am feeling very depressed and weak. I would rather go home.'

'As you wish, Munira. I thought we could offer prayers for the departed souls. Maybe some other time.'

After a few minutes, Munira held Sehmat's hand, drew it closer and whispered, 'Maybe we should go to the mosque and pray for Major Sahib's soul?'

Sehmat was quick to react and instantly directed the driver to the new destination, keeping a check on her own heart that was beginning to beat at a high pace. Half an hour later, the two women stepped out of the car and began climbing the stairs to the mosque. Clad in black burkas, they were covered from head to toe and mixed easily with scores of similarly dressed women. When they reached the last flight, Sehmat requested Munira to proceed ahead while she would run back and fetch flowers from a florist nearby.

Without waiting for the young widow to respond, Sehmat turned and began climbing down the stairs. Amidst screaming hawkers trying their best to outdo each other in selling their wares, Sehmat ordered a large flower basket, paid for it in advance and told the eager seller to keep it ready by the time she returned.

She then rushed to the first available telephone booth. To her dismay, the phone was out of order. Unable to see another public booth in the vicinity, she looked around for a shop from where she could make the all-important call. She almost choked with panic, but then spotted a shop that was manned by an old, uneducated-looking man who was busy sprinkling water on a huge pile of betel leaves. He looked like a priest at the mosque with his attire and long flowing beard. He had a 'couldn't care less' attitude about himself and was curt and precise with customers. Sehmat had no choice but to deal with him and make the best of the prevailing situation.

'May I use your phone, Khan Sahib?' That she was putting an extra effort to appease the shopkeeper was evident from the very first dialogue.

The old man gave a hard stare to the burka-clad woman. His disapproval was blatant. 'Where and who do you want to call?' His tone was sharp and he spoke in chaste Urdu.

'Khan Sahib, my husband was to pick me up but it is already very late. Will you please let me use your phone?'

she said and simultaneously withdrew a five-rupee note from her handbag and handed it over to the kiosk owner. But the old man wasn't done yet. Accepting the currency, which was many times the actual cost of an ordinary call, he retorted, 'Give me the number, I'll try.'

Sehmat had no choice. She hurriedly fished out a small piece of paper from her handbag, scribbled the telephone number of the First Secretary to the Indian Embassy and reluctantly handed it over. The old man dialled each number at the slowest possible pace while keeping an eye on the nervous customer. For a fleeting moment, Sehmat imagined him to be a part of the counter-intelligence network and wondered if the old man was buying time to get her arrested. She was sweating profusely beneath her veil and it had begun to show. The wet thin cloth was stuck to her forehead with sweat beads seeping out of the fabric.

'Hello, who is speaking?' the old man said in a loud, booming tone that attracted the ears of nearby kiosk owners. Sehmat flinched. He waited and listened to the response but it ended abruptly. Replacing the receiver, the old man mumbled harsh words and started dialling again. This time he was greeted with a harsher tone which also ended abruptly.

'What a silly man he is! Starts shouting even before listening to me. No culture, ethics or etiquettes? What kind of a husband do you have, Begum Sahiba?'

'Can I please try, Khan Sahib? I understand my husband well. He must be under a lot of pressure at work. But he'll talk to me.' Sehmat was speaking softly, trying to keep the conversation inaudible to passers-by. The old man thought for a brief moment, scratching his beard at the same time. A few agonizing moments later, he replied, 'Ok, you may try, but don't take long.'

Sehmat grabbed the receiver with both her hands and dialled the number, waiting patiently. The phone kept ringing and the beads of sweat continued to pour, spreading all over the thin veil. Finally a voice came through. It was the First Secretary himself.

'Zulu 405 here. This is an emergency,' she said in rapid-fire English, hoping that the old man would not be able to understand. She simultaneously turned her back and cupped the mouthpiece, making it difficult for the old man or the onlookers to eavesdrop.

Using brief coded words, she fixed a meeting time. She then handed the phone back, thanked the old man and requested him to keep the balance. The old man could barely respond. Sehmat rushed through the crowded lane and reached the florist's kiosk, picked up the basket and ran through the narrow path leading to the stairs of the mosque, to find Munira impatiently waiting for her.

'What took you so long?' Munira asked.

'It was very crowded,' Sehmat responded with a helpless gesture.

On their way back home, Sehmat noticed many police jeeps arriving in quick succession and encircling the crowded market. It became obvious to Sehmat that the intelligence agencies had monitored the conversation and would soon grill the old man. But what impressed her even more was the speed with which the police were able to home in on the source of the phone call.

As the car reached the haveli, Sehmat emerged first and rushed to the other side to help her sister-in-law. Both the women were draped in black veils, but Sehmat's face wore all the signs of nervousness. Mir had categorically restrained her from the steps that she was now taking at regular intervals. Apart from the fear of getting caught, the guilt of having killed two innocent people was also beginning to take a toll on her. It was a feeling of dissolution, and she did not have the luxury of pouring out her sentiments to anyone. Her mind repeatedly raced down memory lane, to the scene of the old man running on the road, pleading to the approaching truck to stop. She tried but could not remove his distressed face from her mind. Her conscience robbed her of every vestige of peace.

On their way to Munira's room, Sehmat almost fainted when her sister-in-law stopped abruptly, turned full circle to face her squarely, and pointedly asked, 'Who were you speaking to on the phone near the mosque?'

Her shocked expression was plainly and clearly visible for even a blind person to see. Thinking quickly on her feet, she pulled herself together, stepped closer and hugged her sister-in-law. She recouped her composure and steadied her beating heart before coming up with a suitable reply. 'I am not well, Munira. Perhaps I am in the family way. I wanted to see my doctor, but could not confide in you due to the prevailing circumstances. I do hope you will appreciate my situation?' Munira looked somewhat convinced and relieved. The two women took each other in a tight embrace and wept.

Minutes later Sehmat was sitting in her room, planning her next move. She had to pass on the information. It was vital for her country to identify the traitors. After making up her mind on the next course of action, she sat down to offer prayers but could not bring herself to focus. Her mind was not at peace. She opened her eyes and murmured, 'I love you, dear Munira, but I had no choice. My country comes first.' Tears continued to roll down her cheeks as she finished praying, unaware that both the betel seller and the florist had been taken into custody by Pakistani intelligence and whisked away to an unknown destination.

14

Iqbal was overwhelmed by the rush of feelings that came over him on hearing the news of Sehmat's pregnancy. The very thought of becoming a father excited him. He owed his growth and rise to Sehmat. He felt like his prayers had been answered. Yet, Mehboob's untimely death had removed the sheen from the excitement, casting a heavy cloud of gloom that refused to lift. He continued to wear a sad face as he received an endless stream of visitors. The courtyard was filled with wreaths of all shapes and sizes. Senior officials, bureaucrats and a host of visitors he had never met before were still lining up to pay homage. Given General Sayeed's rank and position at the ISI, everyone wished to be seen doing so.

Sehmat was restless. She had an agenda on hand. She was also aware that the First Secretary would not be alone. Having monitored the communication, the Pakistani counter-intelligence would tail him and arrest whoever he met. Yet the risk had to be taken. She once again dressed herself in the black burka and prepared to leave. She went up to her husband and said in a hushed tone, 'Iqbal, I want to see the doctor right now. Can you come with me?'

Iqbal gave her a worried look. 'Hope you are okay. Anything urgent?'

'I am fine. I just want to be doubly sure. I have gone through a whole lot of tension and stress.'

'But I can't leave Abba Huzoor alone. I can't leave this place. Unfortunately, I can't even request Munira to accompany you. Could you please go by yourself?'

That was precisely what Sehmat was expecting to hear. Responding quickly, she said, 'I understand, Iqbal. I'll manage. Please take care here. I won't be long.'

She stepped out of the haveli and surveyed the prevailing peace in the neighbourhood. 'It's a matter of time,' she told herself before getting into the rear seat. No one recognized her as her car sped past the visitors. She ordered the driver to proceed without giving any directions. Aslam Khan was an old hand. Having served the Sayeeds for over a decade, he knew that he was supposed to first drive out of the cantonment.

Sehmat had fixed an appointment with her gynaecologist before leaving. The black car came out of the military zone and moved at a steady pace towards the wholesale vegetable market. Sehmat used her make-up kit as a rear-view mirror to check if she was being tailed. Satisfied with this small drill, she directed Aslam to stop near the entrance of the big bazaar.

She alighted from the car and walked straight into a group of burka-clad women so that it would be difficult for anyone following her to catch up.

She emerged at the other end of the market and hired a rickshaw to ferry her to the new destination. The driver was a smart and reckless young man, oblivious to the world around him. He drove at breakneck speed, zigzagging the rickshaw with deft control, and manoeuvred it through the narrow lanes, leaving behind a trail of screaming pedestrians. Without uttering a word, he brought the vehicle to a halt near a grocery shop, accepted the money and melted into the crowd without even caring to look back.

Sehmat entered a large shop and looked around. It was loaded with all kinds of dry fruits, stocks and rations that were neatly stacked in scores of shelves. The shop was fairly big in size and had more attendants than customers. She found, to her surprise, that all of them were busy rearranging the stocks rather than attending to the few customers present inside. No one, therefore, paid attention when Sehmat demanded chickpeas, 8 mm in size.

'No, Madam, we don't have that variety. Maybe you could check at the corner shop. Chickpeas of this size are usually not available and command a premium.' Without waiting for her response, the attendant resumed the job at hand.

'Of course we have them, if you would please follow me, Begum Sahiba.' A soft but firm response from a gentleman who emerged from nowhere shook both the attendant and the customer. From his expressions it was clear that he was the owner himself. The middle-aged, well-built man, wearing a traditional Pathani suit, politely gestured to the burka-clad woman, directing her to the other end of the shop. Sehmat did as she was told and waited while the owner ducked between shelves and fished out a bag containing chickpeas the size of marbles.

Sehmat had never met him before but recognized him from the photographs that Hidayat Khan had shown her. His name was Sarfraz and, according to her father, he could be trusted with any responsibility.

'Could you please tell me how much quantity is available? I need to serve at least 444 people.' 444 was the code that Hidayat had established with Sarfraz. Sehmat hoped it would help her in establishing her identity and waited for the man to respond.

By now the attendant had drifted to other customers. His face wore an expression of fear. Not only was he unaware of the merchandize, he was also caught showing disinterest in his work. He had acquired the job after a great deal of persuasion and effort and was now worried about losing it.

'Is there something so serious, Sehmat, that you had to personally come here?' Sarfraz's one sentence put Sehmat at ease and relief flooded her face.

'Yes, Sarfraz Bhai,' she replied. 'I need this paper to be given to 411. I can't risk going across the street. I would surely be followed, but you'll understand that it's most urgent.'

Sarfraz had helped transferring many similar messages in the past. But after Hidayat's death, this was the first time he had been called upon for such an errand. He took possession of the folded sheet and started putting chickpeas into a paper bag. As he was doing so, he noticed another burka-clad woman approaching Sehmat. Sensing danger, he hurriedly shoved his right hand into his side pocket, firmly gripping the concealed pistol he carried.

'Hi Sehmat, 411 has sent me. Can I have the info? I am in a hurry and need to get out of here. It is getting riskier as we talk.'

It took some time for a bewildered Sehmat to understand the woman's message and deduce her real identity. Sarfraz, though, was quick to follow the developments. He placed the folded sheet of paper with the handwritten instructions at the bottom of the paper bag and filled it with chickpeas.

Handing it over to the woman, Sehmat said, 'Please deliver this info urgently and be careful. The safety of my countrymen is in your hands now.'

'Yes, indeed. But you took a grave risk, Sehmat. They are all over the place. Be careful. I have been told to request you not to communicate with us any more and, if possible, go back to India. If you agree, then leave the lights of your room switched on after midnight tonight.'

Before Sehmat could respond, the woman had already stepped out of the shop and was in the process of sitting in a waiting rickshaw.

Sehmat saw her depart and heaved a sigh of relief, while Sarfraz filled another paper bag. From the woman's voice, it was apparent that she was the First Secretary's wife, Anjali, whom she had met at a party. Sehmat stepped out of the shop and boarded another rickshaw. Later, she walked back to her car.

As they exited the market, Sehmat noticed a vehicle with the Indian flag surrounded by police vehicles. When she looked carefully she saw that in the centre of the commotion was Gaurav Ghei, the First Secretary of the Indian consulate, explaining his presence at the wholesale vegetable market to a large number of Pakistani intelligence officials who looked nonplussed at the long list of groceries in his possession. Sehmat smiled under the cover of her veil.

She soon reached her doctor's residence and chatted with her till she was sure that her tracks were well covered. Dr Huma Siddique was a middle-aged woman. She was respected amongst the elite for being a successful gynaecologist. She had the country's who's who on her list. Though she did not meet patients at her residence, Huma knew that she could not ignore the daughter-in-law of the second in command of the dreaded ISI.

'It's so very kind of you to have taken out the time, Doctor. I was very nauseated and uncomfortable throughout the day. But it appears my worries have vanished by just talking to you,' she said and slung her bag on her shoulder, indicating that she was ready to leave. 'I must get going now. My husband has to resume duty tonight and General Sahib is leaving tomorrow. Thank you once again, Doctor. I appreciate your personal care,' she said smiling.

Huma did not have much to offer. After examining Sehmat, she was sure that there wasn't any reason for her to worry. But she was also sympathetic to Sehmat's emotional stress caused by the two unfortunate deaths in quick succession. 'I understand, Sehmat. It is not easy to cope with what you have been through. Please feel free to call me if you need anything.'

Back in the car, Sehmat rested her tired and aching head on the backrest, planning her next move. She was uncertain of her future and needed time to introspect. Once she was in her room, she threw off her burka and dropped on the bed. But the intercom buzzed before she could close her eyes.

'Sehmat, could you please quickly come to the study?' the General's voice was stained with alarm. Sehmat knew instinctively that there was trouble. Confident that she could not be homed in on, she rushed to the study and saw two officials standing in front of the General. On the table in front lay small pieces of wires, nuts, bolts and the two metal pieces that Sehmat knew were the parts of her listening device. Bloodstains were clearly visible on the pieces that were wrapped in cellophane paper. A note lying on the side accurately identified the pieces as parts of some Morse code equipment.

Feigning ignorance and wearing an expression that almost dismissed the presence of the officials, Sehmat gave her father-in-law a hard but emotional look. 'You shouldn't be working at this hour, Abba Huzoor. You have an early flight tomorrow. All these matters are not more important than your health, especially after what we have gone through.' She then turned her attention towards the officials. 'Would it be possible for you to meet him some other time? Hopefully you'll appreciate that he too needs some rest?'

Sehmat's words were soft but cold and the officers apologized. Their faces fell and they looked embarrassedly at the General, expecting to be dismissed. Despite the tense moment, Sayeed smiled under his breath and waited for their conversation to end. He looked at the officers' tense faces and then at the metal pieces.

'I think there is nothing that can't wait till tomorrow. Anyway, Abdul is not alive to justify the existence of these wires and bolts in his room. I still can't believe he was a traitor. In fact, I can vouch for his loyalty. It nevertheless needs to be fully investigated. Please come and see me in the office sometime next week. And take prior appointment when you do that.'

General Sayeed's words were music to Sehmat's ears, forcing the two officers to beat a hasty retreat. She noticed that her father-in-law was uncomfortable holding the metal pieces in his hand. He realized that his name was being linked to a possible act of treason. He knew for a fact that the intelligence agencies would not have come to his doorstep unless the officials were more than sure of some wrongdoing. Worried, he looked at Sehmat.

'Do you think Abdul could have been involved in some way in this espionage activity?' he asked. Sayeed's eyes shifted skywards as he spoke, thinking of the far-reaching consequences. Sehmat noticed the traces of fear in his voice. He was not an ordinary General and ISI was no run-of-the-mill organization. There was no one in Pakistan, not even politicians, who wasn't scared of the dreaded ISI. Sayeed was more than respected. Being the second in command, he was feared. And here he was, shaken and worried about his reputation.

'No, Abba Huzoor. It is impossible. Not Abdul. Anyone else, but Abdul. Even though he did not quite like me, I can vouch for his integrity and loyalty. Besides, these wires, nuts and bolts could belong to any equipment. These officers just want to justify their existence and earn some brownie points in the bargain. You should have seen their faces. They knew that they were caught on the wrong foot. I can bet this matter won't show up in their files first thing tomorrow morning.'

'I hope so, Sehmat. I sincerely hope so, at least for the sake of our family's reputation,' Sayeed said and stood up, putting his hands on Sehmat's shoulders. 'I have my hands full already. Hopefully, Allah will spare me from further difficulties. Thanks for all your good work. You have come like a blessing from the heavens to our family. I owe all this to my good friend, Hidayat. May his soul rest in peace.'

Sehmat watched him leave and then withdrew to the safety of her room. Entering her bathroom, she closely examined the panels. There were enough telltale signs to put Sehmat in a tight spot. She opened one of the panels and saw electric wires passing through the ceiling. A mysterious smile appeared on her face. She went back to the room and bolted the door from inside.

Half an hour later, when she emerged from the bathroom, her face looked relieved at what she had achieved. The screws were back in place, sealing the cavity from where Abdul had uprooted the Morse code machine. A long cable ran along the side wall, the end of which was fixed to a bracket. A small hairdryer was firmly fixed to the bracket, positioned in such a manner that it hung parallel to the front mirror.

Pleased by her handiwork, Sehmat undressed and stood under the shower. She then commissioned the newly fitted gadget by drying her hair. Tired and relieved at the same time, she fell asleep as soon as she lay down on her bed forgetting to switch off the lights in her room. She was also blissfully unaware of the search squad, led by sniffer dogs, scanning the backyard of the haveli.

Outside, in the chilly autumn air, one of the officers in charge of the search squad stood at the rear doorstep. He was holding the broken tile beneath which Sehmat had planted the duplicate key. With a puzzled look on his face, he inquiringly glanced at his other teammates, seeking an answer. That the tile didn't break on its own was evident from the manner in which it was hammered out. The squad had come to inspect the house of the Deputy Chief of the ISI and that too without his knowledge. And they all knew the consequences of their actions.

After their futile attempts to find any other clue, the squad directed the dogs back to the waiting truck and drove away. Minutes later, a shadow emerged from the bushes across the road. The figure lowered his tiny binoculars, scanned the area and flashed once. Two lights lit brightly, indicating that a big car was now on its way. As it came closer, a small flag fluttering on its right side became visible. The car stopped near the shadow. Without wasting a moment, the man sat in the vehicle which sped in the same direction. As the car picked up speed, its occupant fished out a small radio from below the seat and pressed a button.

'Tango sierra tango, sierra papa,' echoed from the transmitter.

In the safety of a hotel room in the city, two men sat with their headphones, listening and jotting down the transmitted message. While one acknowledged the transmission by releasing a short beep, the other picked up an intercom and pressed the buzzer.

'Yes?'

'Tomorrow same time, same place.'

'Thanks'.

Switching his set off, Mir secured the radio and rested his head on the headrest. 'Go easy, Sehmat, go easy. You are in grave danger now,' he muttered to himself as the car exited the cantonment.

15

Sehmat woke up to the sound of loud knocks on her door. She opened her eyes and immediately looked at the wall clock and then at the brightly glowing bulbs she had left switched on.

'Oh my god!' she exclaimed and rushed to switch them off. She then unlocked the door and pulled the handle of the latch till it rested against the wall. Her vision was still blurred. She hadn't fully recovered from last night's fatigue, and there was carelessness in her body language. Rubbing her eyes gently, she looked up. Major Iqbal Sayeed stood at the entrance in battle gear, with two cups of tea in his hands. 'Good morning, Sehmat. How's this for a surprise?' Iqbal smiled, hoping to cheer her up.

'When did you come and what are you doing in this full rig?' Sehmat didn't seem impressed by his act.

Putting on a brave front, he said, 'I have been given two days special leave. Have to join my battalion thereafter. We are moving to the border. War looks imminent. My Commanding Officer has granted me a short break considering the tragedy in the family. Abba Huzoor has also postponed his departure by a few hours. He's not got over all this as yet.'

'Where's he? Has he woken up?' Sehmat's mind suddenly became alert, exploring different possibilities of what could have gone wrong. Iqbal observed that her face bore expressions of worry.

In an effort to put her at ease, he quickly remarked, 'No, I think he slept very late. He told his Staff Officer to delay his departure. They are all waiting for him to come out.'

'Who are these people?' Sehmat was now struggling hard to keep her composure, fearing that the inquiry on the metal pieces had resurfaced.

'Oh, it's his staff and some outsiders whom I haven't met before. But why do you ask? And may I enter, please?'

'Oh, sure. And thanks for this. I am impressed,' Sehmat said and moved away from the door. 'Yesterday two people came over with some funny metal pieces and a report suggesting that Abdul was possibly involved in some kind of espionage.'

'Involved in what? Abdul? Are they out of their minds?' Iqbal looked visibly shocked. But Sehmat could not help noticing that his expressions were not genuine. She instinctively felt that Iqbal knew more but was feigning ignorance. Her mind began racing. *What are you trying to hide, Iqbal?* But her thoughts died down without translating into words. Instead, she decided to play along.

'That's what I felt and shooed them away. I wonder if they have come again?' Sehmat quipped while carefully observing Iqbal's body language. She was beginning to suspect foul play.

'In that case, would you please get ready quickly and meet these people? They are all sitting in the office. Meanwhile, I'll change.'

While Iqbal unzipped his jacket, Sehmat washed her face and brushed her hair. Just before leaving the bathroom, she switched on the hairdryer and left the bathroom door ajar so that Iqbal could observe the new arrangement. She then walked out, taking brisk and long strides. Her heart was pumping blood, fast enough to give her a haemorrhage. She entered the living room through the back door and glanced at the five people present. She was relieved to see unfamiliar faces.

'Good morning to you all,' she said while taking a hard look at all those present around the large office table. Her face was still tense, but she did not try to put on an act. She felt justified in behaving like a family member who was struggling to come to terms with a horrific tragedy. Stepping closer to the table, she continued in the same vein, 'Sorry to have kept you waiting. I am afraid we are going through some hard times. Hope you all understand. Is there something serious that can't wait?'

There was a sudden movement of chairs in the office as the officials scrambled to stand up at the same time.

'Good morning, err, Madam. Sorry to have come unannounced at this hour. There have been some developments for which we want to see General Sahib immediately. We'll come again if it'll take time. Once again, we are very sorry. Please accept our deep condolences. May Allah grant peace to the departed souls.'

'Thank you. I do not know how long you may have to wait. General Sahib slept very late last night. If you have something to hand over, you may leave it with his Staff Officer. I am sure he will revert to you as soon as he can.'

The visitors looked at each other. From their expressions it was clear that they were unable to decide what to do. To push her argument further, Sehmat looked at the Staff Officer who sprang to attention, waiting for instructions.

'Maybe you could help them in some way?' Sehmat looked at the young Captain who was trying hard to understand the ongoing proceedings. His main role was to assist the General and be like a messenger of sorts. He was a smart officer who did precisely what he was told.

'No, no, Madam,' replied one of the visitors. 'We can show this file only to General Sahib. We have instructions to carry it back after he has gone through the contents. Our chairman has already spoken to the General in this regard and it is with his consent that we have come here.'

'In that case, you can wait till Sayeed Sahib wakes up or you can come again after an hour or so. You can be in touch with the Staff Officer because he is scheduled to leave in a few hours. I am afraid he cannot be disturbed at this point of time as he is not keeping too well and needs rest.'

Sehmat's voice was firm and left an impression of authority in the air. The men looked at each other and then huddled together for an impromptu briefing. Shortly, the oldest amongst them stepped aside and approached Sehmat. 'In that case, may we request you to keep this sealed envelope in your custody and show it to him the moment he wakes up? We are staying at the inspection bungalow not very far from here and will come back. We'll keep in touch with Captain Sahib.'

'Yes, I can do that,' she said and accepted the heavy envelope. She then quickly exited the living room without bothering to look back at the officials. She carried the paper bag to her room and studied the seal. She glanced at the bathroom door from where she could hear the sound of running water and decided not to open the envelope in the room. She walked back into the study and bolted the door from inside. She placed the heavy paper bag on the table and closely examined the seal again. She could not make much of its origin, but her gut feeling told her that whatever it was, it contained vital information.

She decided to take the risk and pulled an armchair closer to the study table. With a hairpin she gently pushed the synthetic layer of glue till the edges parted. Fifteen minutes later, she was going through the contents of the file, her eyes growing wide in disbelief.

She flipped through the annexure twice and repeatedly looked at the enclosed photographs before pushing the material back into the paper bag. She tried to glue back the seal but wasn't very successful. She realized that if anyone took a closer look at the re-pasted end, her game would be up. But her new worry was bigger than simply getting caught.

She pulled open her father-in-law's personal cupboard and placed the envelope under the weight of old books. She then went back to her room and saw Iqbal changing into a new set of clothes. He looked up and smiled faintly before continuing with his routine.

'Who were they?' The tone of Iqbal's question wasn't convincing enough and instead increased her suspicion.

'I don't know. They came to meet Abba Huzoor and will come back later.'

'So you sent them back?'

'What else could I have done? They couldn't have sat in the office forever.'

'Any idea about Abba Huzoor?'

'Still sleeping. Maybe I should wake him up after some time. He must eat something. He had almost nothing the whole day yesterday.'

Iqbal looked at Sehmat appreciatingly, his love for her genuinely etched on his face. Sehmat too could feel the flow of his emotions and smiled in return. However, her mind was still racing to catch up with the possible consequences of what she had just learnt. The intelligence reports had categorically stated that there was a security breach at the haveli. It had reported unexplained transmissions and had attempted to link various jigsaw pieces. It also contained photographs of Gaurav Ghei, the First Secretary to the Indian high commission, talking to suspect agents, as well as of his wife who was extensively captured while talking to people at different locations. What was most worrying was that in one of the pictures, she was shown holding a heavy-looking paper bag.

Sehmat recognized the bag as the one that Sarfraz had handed over to Anjali in her presence. 'Has Anjali been arrested? Has she spilled the beans? Is Sarfraz safe?' Sehmat had no idea but realized that the Pakistani intelligence network had probably uncovered the entire operation. Many lives were at risk and she needed to act, and act fast. However, her judgement was clouded. She recalled what Mir had repeatedly impressed upon her during her short training. As if by magic, the words began to ricochet in her mind. 'Whenever you suspect that your cover is exposed, assume it is so and act accordingly.'

Was it time for her to leave? She could not tell, but somewhere deep inside, she knew that sooner rather than later she would have to seriously consider her escape route. After sacrificing her first love, Sehmat had just begun to settle down. Iqbal wasn't the most brilliant of men, nor was he the sharpest. In fact, he depended completely on Sehmat's advice even for his daily affairs. But he loved her deeply and gave her all the space she needed. Now, because of her actions, the entire family was on the verge of collapse. Somewhere deep within, she was ashamed of what she had done. Tears escaped her eyes as she recalled Abdul's face. The sound of his crackling bones under the truck wheels made her sick.

In the privacy of her bathroom, she wept bitterly, giving vent to her pent-up emotions, and then wiped her face dry. Later she and Iqbal had lunch together in their bedroom, letting the General catch up on his sleep. She then helped Munira pack her bags and escorted her till the gate. On her advice, Munira had decided to spend a few days with her parents at Rawalpindi. An hour later, both Iqbal and Sehmat sat down with General Sayeed. They consoled each other and prayed again. Sayeed tried his best to put up a brave front, but Sehmat knew that he was heartbroken.

She deliberately did not mention the secret file that was delivered in the afternoon. *Some issues should be best left forgotten, owing to unforeseen developments at home,* she told herself.

Soon, the General also left. Despite wearing his uniform, he was far from battle-ready. The stars on his shoulders weighed heavily on him.

After seeing him off at the gate, Sehmat walked back to the house. As she climbed the short steps to the living room, she noticed a convoy of vehicles slowly moving towards the haveli. Instead of stopping at the gate, the vehicles moved past and slowed down as they reached the backyard. A large army truck, fitted with numerous antennae, pulled over while the other vehicles drove well past the haveli before coming to a halt.

Sehmat immediately sensed trouble and rushed to the bathroom. She locked the door behind her, stepped on to the bathtub and peeped through the exhaust outlet. There were three men with dogs on long leashes, inspecting minutely the footprints and leftovers outside the haveli. There were a few civilians too who were busy unloading various kinds of equipment from the vehicles. A young officer, dressed in a crisp uniform, was sitting in the jeep, holding a walkie-talkie close to his ears.

Carefully stepping down, Sehmat pulled the flush, washed her hands and opened the door, only to be startled by Iqbal standing outside.

'What, Iqbal? If you were in a rush, you could have knocked.'

'No, err, actually, I err,' Iqbal fumbled repeatedly but could not complete his sentence.

'What? Is something wrong? You are behaving strangely. Can I be of any assistance?'

'Err, no. Actually, I want to use the bathroom urgently. If you'll please excuse me?'

Sehmat stepped aside, allowing him to enter the bathroom. The sheepish grin on his face told Sehmat everything she wanted to know. She looked around. Her heart was beating at a fast pace. She knew that her game was up. Her mind was now working on her escape route, if at all it was still open. She picked up Iqbal's wallet from the writing table and hurriedly went through the contents. While stuffing the currency notes back, she noticed a small paper between the crisp notes. She pulled it out and read its contents. The seriousness on her face gave way to a strange expression and then she broke into a thin, ruthless smile. She placed the wallet back on the table and waited.

Minutes later, the bathroom door opened. A dishevelled Iqbal stood at the door, his face and hair wet. His eyes suddenly filled with shock and horror. Facing him was Sehmat, holding his revolver in her hand, its muzzle pointing towards his forehead.

16

'Tell me everything you know. And don't involve emotions or use them as blackmail. I am here to do a job for my country. And I will not let anyone come in the way. Not even you.' Sehmat's voice was cold and devoid of feelings.

Shaken beyond words, Iqbal stared at the stranger in front of him. Her threat was real and he began to visualize his own corpse on the floor.

Instructed by Sehmat and numb with shock, he dragged himself towards the chair and sat down. Sehmat tied his hands behind him with neckties and stood in front, still holding the gun. Only this time, it was half-cocked. Iqbal was still in a state of stupor. He loved her hopelessly. Despite her changed status, from his wife to an agent, he still could not bring himself to feel otherwise. He was not only in love with the woman who was betraying his country, he had come to depend on her for his very existence.

His mind was searching for a way through which Sehmat could redeem her actions. With a desperate look of appeal in his sorrowful eyes, he pleaded with her and tried to persuade her. But Sehmat was resolute in her mission. Her eyes had a look of fanaticism for her country. And she wasn't afraid to die.

He tried another tactic. 'You cannot get away, Sehmat. They have taken Munira for interrogation but very soon they will be questioning you. Abba Huzoor has also been told not to leave the station. In fact, he has stepped out to give these guys a safe passage. And my plight is that despite all these developments, I still cannot see you in their hands. Why did you do this?'

Shattered, both emotionally and mentally, Iqbal's eyes were wet and filled to the brim with unshed tears. His voice was heavy and his heart was pounding against his ribs, burdened by the knowledge of the lurking danger ahead. His face was shrouded with fear of the consequences of being married to a spy. The very thought of getting court-martialled made him weak in his knees. Sehmat knew too many secrets. Perhaps more than he could ever imagine. She had access to all sensitive files which were meant for the topmost of the ISI hierarchy and the polity. If court-martialled, the minimum punishment would be death. And the feeling of the ultimate punishment had already begun to sink in.

Unwilling to accept the harsh truth staring him in his face, he was still desperate to save Sehmat from the hands of the ISI. If only he could make her disappear, he wished. But the counter web spun by the Pakistani intelligence was too intricate for Sehmat to escape. After brainstorming and not finding a way out, he blurted, 'Please shoot me, Sehmat. And then kill yourself. At least that way we'll be together.'

Sehmat wasn't listening. It was clear to her that Abdul's closeness to Mehboob had made Munira the prime suspect. In any other case, she too would have been in their custody by now. Perhaps the ISI was in a dilemma on how to take two members of the high-profile family for questioning and had decided to focus on Munira first. She was also sure that soon the military police would come knocking at her door. Reaching for the phone, she snatched the receiver off the cradle. After flipping through the army directory for a few seconds, she dialled the most important number in the cantonment. A brief pause later, a smart and well-trained operator came on the line.

'Good morning, this is General Imtiaz Khan's residence.' The voice was cultured and the operator spoke in refined English.

'My name is Sehmat Sayeed. I am Anwar Khan's teacher. I want to speak to Mrs Imtiaz Khan. This is an emergency.'

'Please hold the line while I connect you, Madam,' responded the operator in a clipped tone. Having connected her before, the operator knew that Sehmat's call would be taken. A short while later a thin, sharp voice came over the earpiece. 'Hello, Sehmat. How are you? Hope everything is all right?' Mrs Suraiya Khan sounded happy to hear her voice. She was oblivious to the latest developments at the Sayeeds'.

'I am fine, Madam, but I want your help urgently. Can I come and meet you right now?' Sehmat was extremely polite, not wanting to convey her nervousness.

'I hope all is well? You sound disturbed.'

'Yes, Madam. Iqbal and I have discovered some things which we feel are of enormous significance. I have to share them with you immediately. Any delay could mean disaster for our family.'

There was an uneasy pause at the other end of the line. Sehmat could sense that the older woman was weighing the pros and cons of what Sehmat had said. She wondered if the wife of the second in command in army would take the bait. She also knew that talking to the first lady in the station would help her buy precious time from the military police who would be listening to every word being said.

'Where are you right now?' Sehmat could barely hear her voice.

'At home, Madam.'

'Okay, you may come right away. Do you have any transport?'

'Err, no, Madam. Abba Huzoor has already left. But I think I'll be able to manage.'

'Please wait, I'll send a car across to get you. It will reach you in a short while.' Saying this, Suraiya put the phone down. Sehmat was thinking quickly, planning her next manoeuvre.

General Imtiaz Khan's bungalow wasn't far from the Sayeeds' haveli, and Sehmat knew that there were standby cars parked outside. But she also knew that travelling in Imtiaz Khan's official car would provide her with the much-needed insurance against the ISI hawks. Twenty minutes later, Sehmat and Iqbal were sitting in a flag car. While leaving, Sehmat noticed more cars and trucks emerging from behind the barricade and driving towards the rear entrance of the bungalow. The noose was beginning to tighten. Would she be arrested on her return, she wondered.

'So far, so good,' she muttered as she sat in the rear seat and rested her head on a cushion. Iqbal was tenser than ever. He had no clue about the role he was to play in the ongoing proceedings. Going to the residence of the senior-most Army General without being called was a contravention of military orders. He looked at Sehmat pleadingly, his eyes filled with questions and fear, but he did not say anything.

'It's simple, Iqbal,' Sehmat began as soon as the attendant closed the door of the car. The driver walked towards his seat, giving her a few precious moments. 'You did not have any knowledge about the whole matter. Whatever I say to Mrs Khan would be the gospel truth for you as well. Remain silent and speak only when spoken to. Restrict yourself only to what you will hear me say. To start with, it was Abdul, right from day one. The rest is history. And remember, I will not hesitate to take extreme steps if I am forced to.' After finishing her short, well-rehearsed brief, she paused to see her husband's reaction. Iqbal understood the meaning of her threat. He had seen her putting the gleaming colt in her handbag.

Minutes later, Sehmat was sitting across from Mrs Khan, confidently explaining Abdul's possible involvement in the suspected espionage at the Sayeeds' residence. She forcefully stressed the threat to Munira's safety and repeatedly urged Mrs Khan to intervene.

'She has just lost her husband, Madam. She should at least be allowed to mourn in peace,' she pleaded, leaving strains of emotion floating in the air.

Mrs Suraiya Khan was a seasoned lady. She knew army regulations as much as she understood her limitations. Sehmat's request was beyond her powers even though she could connect to and sympathize with Munira's plight. Besides, she was unsure of whom to speak to regarding this unusual request. On the other hand, Sehmat's initiative at her grandson's school concert was weighing on her mind. She also had an inflated ego that would suffer a steep fall if she failed to exert her clout as the wife of the most powerful army officer in the country. Prompted by Sehmat, she decided to take up the matter in her capacity as the vice chairperson of the Army Officers' Wives Welfare Association.

She picked up the receiver, dialled a number and asked for Lieutenant General Izaz Mirza, the chief of ISI. Mirza quickly came on the line and exchanged polite courtesies. He owed his present appointment to the closeness he enjoyed with the Khans. There was some hesitation in Mrs Khan's voice in the beginning, but as the discussion proceeded, she took complete control.

'Mirza Sahib, I would like to bring to your attention a possible case of high-handedness shown by the army personnel. I have been given to understand that General Sayeed's elder daughter-in-law has been picked up by the military police on some issues related to espionage. It is indeed a very serious charge but I would appreciate if you could personally look into it and ensure adequate safety for the lady. As you would be aware, her husband died of a heart attack just two days ago. I am sure we can be more humane in our approach, even if there is a genuine case against her. May I request you to see that she is treated well and sent home as soon as possible?'

She spoke without offering a break to the General. Then she promptly hung up, leaving the not-so-amused General holding the receiver in his hand. Her message was clear and, even in his position of authority, Lieutenant General Mirza knew that he could not afford to antagonize the wife of the most powerful man in the Pakistani army. Besides, General Imtiaz Khan was also closely related to the Army Chief and he himself had benefited from their relationship. He knew about the Sayeeds' espionage episode and had personally signed the order papers for investigation.

Munira's arrest had not been easy either. Her father was a retired Lieutenant General, and she too carried sufficient clout. It was only after his deputy, General Sayeed, agreed to the line of action that the ISI moved further. Having already questioned Munira to a certain extent, the ISI chief decided to put the issue on the back-burner for the time being.

Sehmat spent the next half hour in a more relaxed state of mind. Having achieved her short-term goal, she quickly drifted to other subjects, easing the tension that had built up in the room. It became evident to Iqbal that both women had enormous admiration for each other. Soon Anwar became the subject of their discussion, with Sehmat outlining his hidden qualities such as determination and a sense of focus. Mrs Khan appeared pleased and in turn complimented Sehmat on her creative teaching style.

Sitting in the corner as a mute spectator, a scared Iqbal wondered about the extent to which his wife had made inroads into the first family. The ease with which Sehmat wielded influence, even in matters concerning national security, shocked him. But in all this destruction, he could see a way out for Sehmat. He observed that Mrs Khan could not even begin to see the web that was being spun by her. Yet, he was also hoping that Sehmat would be able to pull off the plan that she had in mind. He loved her and she mattered to him, even if she was an enemy agent.

Iqbal accepted the teacup that was offered to him by a uniformed butler. He was about to take the first sip when he heard Sehmat seeking Mrs Khan's permission to take Anwar to their haveli for a short while. Shocked, he nearly spilled the tea. The far-reaching consequences of Sehmat's request were clear to him in the very first instant.

'We are extremely depressed, Madam,' he heard his wife say. 'I too am in the family way and my doctor has categorically told me to exercise caution. Anwar's presence would cheer me up a great deal,' Sehmat continued carefully, without a hint of desperation in her voice.

Iqbal wished to scream, 'No!', but could not muster enough courage. Mrs Khan, on the other hand, appeared pleased by Sehmat's request, happy that her grandson would be able to spend quality time with his favourite teacher. Anwar too was very fond of her. When asked, he jumped at the idea of spending a few hours with his teacher at her residence. Ten minutes later, they left in the same car. Sehmat now had a willing hostage in her custody, just in case.

By the time they reached home, Munira had arrived and locked herself in her room. The soldiers at the haveli too were hastily loading their equipment into the waiting trucks, while the fleet of inspection vehicles had begun to pull away. The dogs were no longer sniffing around the haveli and the truck with surveillance equipment had downed its shutters. It was clear that Suraiya's words had worked. However, Sehmat was still extremely uncomfortable. She wasn't entirely sure of how Iqbal would react and therefore kept him within pistol range at all times.

17

As the sky dusked, a flag car approached the newly erected barrier in the cantonment. The driver rolled down his windowpane and brought the car to a halt. The security guards saluted in unison before one of them stepped up to take an identification check.

'Major General Bashir Ahmad Sahib,' indicated the driver while flashing his ID card. The young soldier had barely taken a look at the card when a crisp, husky voice from the back seat threw him off guard. 'Which road will take us to General Sayeed's residence?' it asked. Springing to attention, the guard hurriedly returned the card to the driver and pointed in the direction of the haveli.

The guard was well aware of the reason behind the sudden spurt in high-profile visits to that part of the cantonment. Since the tragedy, excessive VIP movement had kept them on their toes. The guard stepped back smartly and continued pointing in the direction of the house with his right hand while the other three stood to rigid attention.

'First turn left, then turn right and again first turn left, Sir. It's the last bungalow, Sir.'

'Thanks.' The driver changed gears and stepped on the gas pedal almost immediately.

Mir, who was sitting in the back seat, readjusted his peak cap and pressed a tiny button beneath the armrest. This was a signal for the commando who was hiding in the boot and holding an automatic rifle. Despite lying crouched in the cramped space and sweating profusely, his face reflected signs of relief.

The guards at the gate stopped the car before allowing it to move into the portico. The driver sprinted out and opened the rear door. Mir, smartly dressed in a Major General's uniform, stepped out, holding a bouquet of flowers in his right hand. He was aware of Sayeed's absence, yet he had taken precautions. He adjusted the small pistol strapped to his ankle. He waited for a while in the hall before the servant ushered him to the drawing room.

An emotionally wrought and mentally drained Iqbal received Mir, accepted his condolences and thanked him for the kind gesture. He had too much going on in his life to ask for the visitor's details. Instead, he wanted the guest to leave soon. The visitor, though, didn't appear to be in any mood to oblige. After paying his condolences, the General surprised Iqbal by requesting an audience with Sehmat.

'You see, Iqbal, your good lady also happens to be one of the finest teachers around. I hear great stories about her from my grandson. Since I have come this far, I thought I would meet her for a while. It is a loss for the school that she has decided to give up teaching.'

Iqbal was left speechless. He was aware that Sehmat was listening to the conversation. The enormity of her influence was pushing him deeper into depression.

Standing behind the curtain, Sehmat monitored the conversation. She had recognized Mir from a distance. She stuffed the gun into her handbag and stepped into the hall. Poker-faced, she bowed gently and looked at Iqbal, as if seeking his permission to remain present. Without waiting for his reply, she occupied the chair that was placed slightly behind her husband's. She could now observe the two men without being in Iqbal's direct sight. Mir sprang out of his seat and bowed, keeping his eyes focused on the couple.

Mir began his conversation by offering condolences and went on to appreciate her work as a teacher. 'It might not be the right occasion, I am afraid, but I just could not stop myself from thanking you for doing us a big favour. Notorious as he was, my grandson has reversed one hundred and eighty degrees. I would like to compliment you and hope you will continue to guide children, especially in their formative years.'

Mir's eyes were focused on Sehmat, trying to extract whatever information he could from her remarkably composed face. Finding none, he pulled out a small note from his trouser pocket and handed it over to Sehmat. 'He has written a small letter for you, expressing his grief over your family's loss.'

Sehmat took the note and read its contents while Iqbal watched her face from his seat. It was a small but precise note indicating the steps she had to take to facilitate her escape. After reading and absorbing its contents, Sehmat folded the paper and handed it back to Mir.

'Please thank Riaz for such kind words. It is very sweet of him. Maybe you should have brought him along.'

'Oh! He wanted to come and meet you. But this was not an appropriate time. Perhaps on some other occasion. Right now he is with his parents.'

'Riaz is one of my favourite students. I wonder if I could meet him tonight? Iqbal and I are going to the city with another student, Anwar Khan, General Imtiaz Khan's grandson. We hope that the company of children will help us recover from the depression and gloom. He could come with us for a short while.'

'That would be great. He would love to spend some time with you. Though I am flying back in a while, my daughter-in-law will take him there. I am afraid it will have to be for a very short time.'

Sehmat looked at Iqbal who remained motionless and non-committal. He wasn't even aware of Sehmat's plan to visit the shopping plaza. Presuming his silence to be affirmative, Sehmat continued. 'All right, General, in three hours from now, we'll meet near "Cross Plaza".'

'Thanks, Mrs Sayeed. You always take time out for the little ones. That's what makes you so special and loved by the children. And that's how you have won so many hearts. Thank you once again.' Mir stood up, causing Iqbal to spring into action. He rushed to the door and flung it open for the General to exit. Mir shook hands with Iqbal. Before sitting in the car, he took a quick glance at the surroundings and then sank into the plush cushions.

Mir was amazed at Sehmat's performance. She had surpassed his expectations and had complete control over the situation. There was no fear in her voice; she was full of confidence and was calling the shots. Her decision to meet

Mir at 'Cross Plaza' later in the evening showed the authority she wielded at the Sayeeds'. Even her husband, Iqbal, appeared to be in awe of her and was reduced to a mere spectator at the large haveli. 'Well done, Sehmat, God bless you!' Mir uttered. He knew that she was very close to being exposed. His own visit to the haveli was a drastic step he was forced to take in order to execute the rescue operation. He hoped Sehmat would follow his instructions strictly. The tiniest of mistakes could ruin the plan and endanger numerous lives.

The markets lit up as darkness began to set in. Dressed in local Pathani attire, Mir sat in a small open restaurant, watching the movement of the pedestrians across the road. A few of his hand-picked agents kept watch at different positions, waiting for Sehmat to arrive. She walked in on schedule, wearing a burka that covered her from head to toe. Mir was able to recognize her as she was accompanied by a nervous Iqbal who looked handsome in a blue blazer.

There was no sign of Anwar. The two stopped outside the shopping area and briefly spoke to each other before entering the well-lit market. Sehmat was scheduled to exit from the rear end of the plaza from where she was to be picked up by Mir's agents and transferred to a safe location. Mir sighed with relief. All was going according to plan. He lifted his teacup and glanced at one of his men, signalling for the escape car to position itself.

Suddenly his trained eyes spotted Pakistani agents. In an effort to be inconspicuous, the Pakistani counter-intelligence personnel had donned loose-fitting dark-coloured Pathani suits. Yet they stood out in the crowd due to their physique, short hair and the extra alertness in their body language.

Their eyes were scanning the area occasionally but remained focused on Sehmat. There was a distinctive pattern in their movement that kept Sehmat and her husband within striking range. From the slight bulge in their shirts, it was evident that they were carrying small firearms. Observing their movements carefully from a distance, Mir noticed more agents forming an outer ring, frequently conversing on walkie-talkies.

Mir weighed the pros and cons and realized that Sehmat's escape would mean losing many innocent lives and, therefore, had to be abandoned. Reluctantly, he thrust his right hand into his side pocket and pressed the transmitter button thrice. Not too far away, two of his agents looked at their tiny monitors. Their orders were clear; but they looked bewildered and unsure and walked across the road to take a confirmation from their boss. They saw him nod imperceptibly and quickly returned to their positions at the exit door. They then signalled their contact inside the mall.

As the Pakistani agents neared Sehmat, a small poisonous dart hit her in the neck. She fell on the spot, crashing into the entire row of groceries arranged on the shelves. The Pakistani agents stopped dead in their tracks. They were stunned and took a moment to recover from the unexpected turn of events. Belatedly scrambling to their senses, they scattered around the complex, attempting to trace the source of the attack. Minutes later, an explosion inside the shopping arcade shook the entire building, causing a near stampede as shoppers ran towards the exit for safety.

The ensuing melee helped Mir and his agents to leave the site. Before getting into the car, he turned towards the shopping arcade. The bomb had exploded near Sehmat, sending her flying towards the shelves. She must have died instantly, he realized, but could not bring himself to imagine her body being blown into unrecognizable shreds of flesh. The very thought turned his stomach.

Sehmat was like a daughter to him. Fighting a sense of dread, he thought about Tej and what he would tell her. He went over the entire exercise in his mind and wondered if his well-rehearsed plan had leaks that he, a seasoned intelligence officer, had failed to detect. He muttered abuses and deeply regretted failing to save Hidayat's only child. The escape cars converged in a colony on the outskirts of the city. The lanes of the colony were not well-lit, and so, allowed the passengers to get into the safe house without being noticed by neighbours.

Huddled together in the large living room with his team shortly after, Mir took stock of the situation. War was inevitable. The Pakistani leadership had the surprise element on its side, and was confident of causing a serious setback to India. On that account alone, Sehmat's efforts had been a great success. But Mir's mind wandered back to Tej. What would he say to her? How would he break the news to her?

A dark gloom descended in the room. Sehmat had been their most valuable asset. She had to be blown to pieces by her own people so that she could be saved from falling into alien hands. She had served her country selflessly, without raising an eyebrow. Not once did she flinch at the danger and risks to her life. She knew the importance of the entire mission. She had remained committed to the cause and died unsung, soon to be forgotten by both the nation and its people.

Mir held his head between his hands and shut his eyes tight to block the disturbing scene from returning to his mind but failed miserably. Her image kept hounding him again and again. 'I am sorry, dear Sehmat, but we had no choice,' he said to himself repeatedly, his eyes moist with tears.

There was a hushed silence in the house. None of the officers present had ever seen their boss so close to a breakdown. They were sitting silently like mourners beside a corpse, unable to utter a word. Suddenly, the sharp clang of the doorbell, followed by another, threw them out of their seats, breaking their reverie.

They sprang into action, drawing their guns and preparing to shoot down the intruder. They were not expecting visitors. 'Who could it be?' they asked each other. They had carefully picked this particular safe house, away from prying eyes, in order to carry out the operations without being interrupted.

Mir looked at his men and spoke through clenched teeth. 'This could be a serious call. Kill as many or shoot yourself. No one surrenders. If you falter, remember Sehmat and her sacrifice.'

The doorbell rang again, more urgently than the first time. It was louder, indicating that the visitor had no intention of leaving. Mir reached for the door and looked through the peephole. The grip on his pistol eased and the gun dropped to the floor. His tense face dramatically gave way to an expression of joy. Removing the safety chain, he unlocked the door and threw it open. Standing at the entrance, with the black burka slung over one hand, was Sehmat. Like the Mona Lisa, she wore a mysterious smile on her face.

Mir held her by her shoulders and pulled her in before latching the door. Stepping inside, she gave a bemused look to the men who were beginning to emerge from the shadows.

She was a vision. She was alive. She was back and safe. Mir could now go back to India and face his dearest friend's wife.

'So this is what you call a safe house. Great. Now when can I leave for my home, my India?'

Mir's beaming face was like a stream of sunshine in a dark tunnel. Sehmat looked at her mentor, her dark-blue eyes saying it all. She was herself surprised to be alive. She was glad that she had done her duty to the best of her ability and survived the test of time. And now she wanted to return to the safety and warmth of her watan.

Mir's expression suddenly clouded over. How did she manage to cheat death? And how did she find them, especially when she had no knowledge of the safe house?

Sehmat read Mir's thoughts. 'Well,' she explained, 'I didn't accompany Iqbal to the plaza. It was Munira who went with him. This was Iqbal's idea. He was informed by his father that I was going to be arrested. But the General did not want the arrest to take place at his own haveli. Munira accompanied Iqbal because she was told that Mrs Suraiya Khan wanted to meet her. Anwar's presence removed any suspicion that she might have had. Anwar was left behind in the car in the custody of the driver who was told to drive him back home.'

'When Iqbal and Munira, who was clad in a burka, left the haveli, I followed them and saw the explosion from a distance. I saw you escaping in the getaway car soon after the blast. It was easy for me to tail your car, but I faced some difficulty once you entered the colony. Thereafter, it was my spy instincts, some common sense and a bit of luck that helped me locate your so-called safe house. After all, I am no less a spy than you, am I? Now when can you send me to my watan?' Sehmat ended her monologue on a triumphant note, to the cheer and smiles of all present. They were astounded by her display of grit and determination. Their expressions were filled with high respect. She was one of them, yet had far exceeded their expectations.

Words were insufficient. 'Soon, very soon you'll be home,' was all Mir could manage as he gathered her in a tight embrace. Tears were now beginning to roll down his cheeks. But he did not care.

18

An air force transport plane touched down at the Delhi airport landing strip and taxied till it reached the VIP parking bay. Security forces cordoned off the area as soon as the aircraft came to a complete halt. A red carpet was rolled out with alacrity well before the door of the plane opened. An army brass band smartly marched into the enclosure playing 'Jai Bharati' and elegantly halted by the side of the dais that had been temporarily erected to felicitate the arriving VIP.

As if controlled by a remote, their heads turned left in unison. Their gleaming boots moved rapidly to the matching rhythm of the drummers till they all fell into a formation. They came to a halt as the drumbeats stopped. Their heads were now aligned, awaiting the next order. The stage was set with military precision for the war hero.

An accommodation ladder had been manually pushed towards the aircraft. Mir emerged first. He was wearing dark glasses and a black woollen overcoat. He stood briefly on the ladder and scanned the small gathering of high-level officials that had come to receive the special guest. Spotting a frail lady amongst the crowd, he waved, encouraging the middle-aged woman clad in a stark white sari to step out of the huddle. Sehmat, meanwhile, emerged from the aircraft and saw her mother slowly walking towards the ladder. Holding the side rail, she quickly stepped down and ran into her mother's waiting arms. The two wept uncontrollably and remained in a tight embrace. There were tears of happiness, of reunion after a long separation. Loud clapping from the welcome party finally separated the two. Tej cupped Sehmat's face in her hands and took a closer look at the battle-weary eyes. She kissed Sehmat's cheeks before turning to face the officials who had by then lined up on the edge of the red carpet.

As Sehmat walked past the officials, she was showered with rose petals and offered bouquets. She did not personally know anyone in the crowd but graciously accepted their greetings. Holding her mother by the shoulder, she moved past the gathering till she saw something familiar. Sehmat walked away from the laid path and came face-to-face with the fluttering tricolour. Without bothering about the assembled people who were watching her with amazement and curiosity, she knelt down and placed her head on the tarmac. Tears trickled down from Sehmat's eyes. She kissed the cemented floor and whispered, 'Oh my dear Motherland, how I missed you. Thank you for having me back.'

The bandmaster was an old sergeant who had gone through the drill of according ceremonial reception to hundreds of dignitaries. He did not know Sehmat's background but his experienced eyes were quick to realize that she was unique. As if on cue, he swung his baton sideways, bringing the band to an abrupt halt. Coming to attention simultaneously, he swung his hands in the air in quick succession, signalling his band to switch to a new beat. Moments later, the band was playing the national anthem. Sehmat stood up slowly and faced the dais. She was alone on the tarmac, standing tall and saluting the tricolour. She was back home, amongst her own people and in the safety and warmth of her own country.

Sehmat folded her hands in acknowledgement as the band finished playing the anthem. Hard as she tried, she could not hide her tears. She went back to the carpeted track and began receiving bouquets and garlands till she reached the end of the row. She noticed a familiar pair of hands holding a bunch of her favourite yellow roses. She instantly recognized the fingers that were holding the stems ever so gently. She had held those hands before. Her heartbeat quickened as she looked up to face the tall and handsome figure.

'Welcome home, Sehmat,' she heard Aby saying, his words filled with emotion.

The bouquets fell from her hands and scattered on the ground. She buried her head in Aby's broad chest and sobbed uncontrollably.

'You have no idea how much I have missed you, Sehmat. I am proud of you. The whole country is.' Aby's voice conveyed immeasurable pride. She smiled faintly but failed to control her sobs. Memories of another life came rushing back to her.

Aby escorted her to the table on the dais for felicitations and came back to where Tej was standing. Mir watched her from a distance with moist eyes. He was happy to see Sehmat getting back into the fold of her loved ones. Taking the podium, he looked at Tej and wondered if he could even think of doing what the Khans had done for the country. He felt uncomfortable deep within. It dawned on him that while he could sacrifice himself a hundred times, he would find it difficult to send his children into the jaws of death.

'Ladies and gentlemen,' he began, 'It is my esteemed privilege and honour to present to you a family that has set the highest standards of loyalty and dedication in service of our beloved country. Ordinary mortals like us would find it difficult to even think about what my late friend Hidayat and his patriotic family actually did for us. His daughter, Sehmat, went a step further and nearly sacrificed herself to fulfil his dreams. I have no words to describe the raw courage with which she steadfastly fulfilled her duty.' Mir paused briefly. His mind went numb, his words dying on his lips. He could not stop himself from comparing his sense of loyalty with that of the Khans. Clearing his throat, he continued, 'Before I proceed further, I would like to invite on stage the woman without whose encouragement and active participation Sehmat would not have succeeded in her mission.' Mir stopped briefly again and turned his head towards Tej. Aby ushered Tej on to the stage amidst loud applause.

Stepping away from the podium, Mir walked to the edge of the stage and escorted Tej to the seat next to Sehmat. He was about to go back to the podium when he noticed something unusual: Sehmat was sliding from her seat. Mir realized that she was fainting. He turned immediately and caught Sehmat by her shoulders before she collapsed. He lifted her in his powerful arms and rushed to a waiting ambulance with Tej and Aby in tow. They were soon on their way to the military hospital at the Delhi cantonment.

An hour later, an army doctor emerged from the examination room to face the three tense people. He smiled at them reassuringly and walked up to Tej. His smile widened as he came closer. 'Your daughter is fine. There is absolutely nothing to worry about. It was fatigue, nervousness and excitement that caused the blood to rush to her head. She'll be fine soon. All she needs is rest.'

'But doctor, why did she faint?' Tej still looked worried, apprehending bad news from the doctor.

'She did not faint, Madam, well, not exactly. But she has to be careful and, as I said earlier, she needs rest. I presume you know that she is pregnant?'

Tej covered her open mouth with both her hands, her eyes expressing extreme shock. Unable to regain control over her emotions, she slumped towards Mir who let her head rest on his shoulder.

'How much more suffering will my daughter undergo?' she wondered aloud. 'Will she be able to bear this cruel twist of fate?' Mir had no answer.

Aby was standing nearby. Moving a step closer, he put his arm around Tej and gently pulled her away from Mir. He wiped her tears and made her sit on a bench a few steps away. Squatting by her side, he held her trembling hands firmly and looked at her as if nothing unusual had happened.

'Look, Mrs Khan, there is nothing to feel bad about. She was married and a child is always a blessing. She has lost her husband, but if you and Sehmat agree, I will be honoured to have her as my life partner.'

Even from a distance, Mir could understand what Aby was saying by reading his lips. He came closer and held him tightly in an embrace. 'I must have done something great in my previous life to see the finest display of human spirit. I am proud of you, Aby. I am really proud of you, my son. May God bless you.'

'Don't make me a martyr, Sir. I have loved Sehmat right from the day I first saw her. I still do, and hope that she will agree to be my wife.'

The expressions of depression and defeat evaporated from Tej's face. Tears of happiness streamed down her face. She hugged Aby, clutching him with her feeble arms. She was happy that Sehmat would be able to pick up the pieces of her broken life and start afresh from where she had left. She deserved a new chance at a happy life with the man she truly loved. The army doctor escorted Tej to the room where Sehmat was resting after the check-up. Mir and Aby, meanwhile, sat on the bench outside and accepted tea served by a smartly dressed orderly.

Wiping her tears, Tej patted down her hair and opened the door to Sehmat's room. She was lying on the bed. She watched her mother enter and close the door behind her. Their eyes met, and they exchanged bittersweet smiles that reflected the pain they had gone through. Sehmat hid the fact that she already knew about her pregnancy from Tej. She was happy to be a mother, but the reality of having killed so many innocent people had begun to take its toll on her. Tej could almost read her mind.

'Congratulations,' she said sitting by her bedside. 'I know how you feel, but I have good news for you. Aby still loves you and wants to marry you.'

'But, Mother, I am carrying Iqbal's child and under no circumstances am I going to get an abortion.'

'He knows everything, but he says he loves you irrespective of that and just wants your consent.'

Sehmat was nonplussed for a moment. The chance of being with her first love was exciting but deep within she was depressed. Would she ever be able to marry again and live happily after taking so many innocent lives?

'I need some time, Mother. At the moment, I am not in a state to take such a decision. Also I don't want to go back to Srinagar. Could you help me settle down in Maler Kotla?'

'Maler Kotla? Where is that? And why there?' Tej's voice was tinged with the same surprise that was written on her face.

'It is Abdul's home town,' Sehmat replied with a sorrowful expression.

'And who is Abdul?' Tej began to get more worried.

'He was the most faithful servant of the Sayeeds.'

'But that was in Pakistan, Sehmat. You are now back in your own country.'

'Yes, Mother, but my conscience is heavy with guilt. Maybe this way I shall be able to ease some of its burden. I hope Abdul will forgive me for what I did to him.'

'And what did you do?'

'I crushed him under a military truck.'

Tej was shocked by Sehmat's plain speaking. She began to realize the extent of trauma her daughter was carrying in her mind and heart. She held Sehmat's hands firmly and kissed her forehead. 'I can understand what you must be going through. But remember, what you did was for the sake of your country. And I am with you, always.'

'Thank you, Mother,' she said, as she shut her eyes and pushed her head into the soft pillow. Tej could see the pain on her face but could do little to ease her agony.

'Only time can heal her wounds and ease her burden,' she told herself.

As she came out of the room, she looked at the two men. Their eyes were glued to her face, trying to read her expressions. She smiled and walked slowly towards them. She was in a dilemma as she did not have the courage to face Aby. She sat next to Mir and, without looking directly at Aby, asked, 'Where exactly is Maler Kotla?'

Mir immediately realized that all was not well. Tej told them what Sehmat had said and they listened in silence. It took Mir no time to understand what Sehmat was going through. Anyone else in this situation would have become a nervous wreck. But what surprised him was the calmness and fortitude with which Aby took it all in his stride.

As he walked towards his car an hour later, Aby's words still rang in his mind. 'Don't worry, Mom, I am even more determined. And I'll wait for eternity if so needed. Our first priority is to get her back to normality. She must be cheerful in her condition.'

His calling her 'Mom' wasn't missed by Tej. It cheered her up and also kept her hope alive.

19

Admiral M.S. Chand, Chief of the Naval Staff (CNS) of the Indian Navy, was pacing up and down in the 'operations room' at the naval headquarters (NHQ) in New Delhi. His face wore a worried expression. There was pin-drop silence in the hall that seated more than a dozen other Admirals who were waiting patiently for their Chief to speak. Chand had arrived before the scheduled time of the meeting, and had waited for everyone to assemble and take their seats. One by one, the officers had entered the hall, saluted the Chief and occupied their respective seats. Each officer had checked his watch to confirm if he had arrived on time because it was such a rare sight to see the CNS coming much ahead of schedule.

'Gentlemen,' began the CNS, after taking a long look at the officers, 'in comparison to the Indian Army, the navy is yet to prove its mettle. We are one-tenth the size of the army and relatively untested on the battlefield. While the air force has repeatedly demonstrated itself through sheer air power and vital support to the country's defence, the navy more or less stands in isolation due to its perceived limited role. Some people in the bureaucracy tend to accord it step-motherly treatment when it comes to formulating battle strategies. And it hurts even more when those in power overlook the navy's views at high-level meetings. I am also deeply perturbed by their apprehensions of the navy's limited capability in a war. But I am determined to press our case directly to the political leadership. Please be prepared. The navy is going to play an active role in safeguarding the interests of our great nation.'

The CNS paused for a brief moment. He had his own reasons to press the navy's case. Intelligence reports had categorically confirmed the presence of Pakistani submarines, primed to launch an all-out attack on India's lone aircraft carrier, INS Vikrant, in Indian waters.

Compounding the Chief's worries was the fact that Vikrant was not fully operational. Having developed cracks in its main boiler, the big hulk's ability to catapult fighter aircraft into flight had become suspect. Moreover, the Indian Navy could barely provide enough escort ships which were needed for carrier operations at sea in a hostile situation.

Chand walked up to the wall and began positioning various models of ships on the huge chart. Holding Vikrant's tiny replica in his hand, he turned to face his audience. 'Any damage to the flagship would not only cause us humiliation, it would also adversely damage the morale of our men. Reports suggest that there are at least four Pakistani submarines in our waters, including the US-built Ghazi. The other subs are just as dangerous. They are equally advanced French machines that are capable of eluding us. While on one hand the navy has to keep Vikrant out of harm's way from the sub attack, on the other hand, we have to engage in a diplomatic tussle with our own babudom.'

Placing the model ship on the table, the CNS took his chair and put his head against the cushion. The meeting went on till midnight and the members dispersed only after the data to be presented to the government was compiled. It was rare for the officers to see their CNS involving himself in the minutest of details. The first battle was within the system; to convince the political leadership of the navy's worthiness to take on the enemy. It was not going to be easy, but Chand was not one to give up.

Armed with statistics and data, the CNS went to the Defence Minister the following day. The bureaucrats in the defence ministry persisted with their version of the unfolding scenario which was short-sighted. 'Given the Pakistani naval strength,' Chand was told, 'they can do little at sea that can harm India's vast coastline. Over 80 per cent of the Indian trade carried over the sea is conducted by foreign shipping liners. Pakistanis would think twice before attacking any foreign vessel and earning the wrath of the Western powers,' the bureaucracy opined.

Chand was shocked and dismayed by their comments. 'What do you know about war?' he wished to ask them but decided to push the matter through with persistence instead. The stakes were too high. Being the navy's Chief, it was his duty to stand up to the challenge, both within and outside, and yet emerge victorious.

To an audience that was to take the final call, Chand presented a detailed report on Pakistan's inventory and its intentions. He placed copies of the intelligence report before the Prime Minister in the war room, and drew her attention to the specifics and statistics.

'Madam,' he pleaded before the Prime Minister, 'Pakistanis have Ghazi on wet lease from the US and Daphne-class subs from the French. In addition, they have acquired midget submarines and chariots. These units are best suited for both long-drawn operations and for clandestine attacks. We have to consider the fact that they can attack ships in harbour and damage vital installations. I understand that the Pakistani Air Force is closely coordinating with its navy for the singular mission of damaging our aircraft carrier. We cannot let this happen. And the only way to defend it is by allowing us to counter-attack.'

The Prime Minister heard him patiently but did not respond. Instead, she looked questioningly towards the bureaucrats, seeking an explanation from them but they seemed in no mood to relent. Even though most of them had never ventured into the sea, they felt they were experts in the field of naval warfare.

'But, Admiral,' one of them argued, 'given Pakistan's strength on the West Coast, how do you feel they'd be able to penetrate so deep? Let's look at their firepower.' Rising from his chair, the senior bureaucrat went on to read a prepared text. He felt it was his time to make a lasting impression on the Prime Minister, who was patiently listening to the discussion.

'Let's examine what the Pakistani Navy possesses in terms of numbers,' he continued, simultaneously placing a leather folder marked 'Secret' in front of the PM. He then went on to read the names of Pakistani ships and submarines.

'Madam,' he said gently, 'on paper, Pakistan has the following on its west coast:

1. One cruiser, the Babur
2. Four destroyers, the Shah Jahan, the Badr, the Khaibar and the Alamgir
3. Three Daphne-class submarines, the Shushuk, the Hangor and the Mangro
4. One frigate, Tipu Sultan
5. One survey vessel, Zulfiqar
6. Eight minesweepers
7. Two motor torpedo boats
8. Two tankers, the Attock and the Dacca
9. One tug, an assortment of twelve midget submarines, twelve chariots and two seaward defence boats.'

Then he turned to his right to face the CNS. 'Admiral, are you sure that, with such limited naval capability, Pakistan would dare to come anywhere near our coast? Besides, do you think that by sending our navy out into the blue waters, we will be able to stop the British fleet or the US carriers or for that matter the Russian battleships from operating off our coast?'

He then glanced towards the PM to see her reaction. Finding none, he looked at his counterparts from the ministry and saw them directing sarcastic smiles at the CNS. The bureaucrats as usual were at war with their uniformed counterparts.

'But what about the Ghazi?' the CNS was about to ask when he noticed the PM getting up. She looked at the Army Chief and then glanced at the Chiefs of the intelligence bureau, home affairs and air force. 'Do you gentlemen have anything to add?' Her question was an indication that she had had enough of their war games. Getting no response, she looked at her watch and then at the CNS. 'Admiral, do you have anything to say?'

Bruised and snubbed, the Admiral walked through the long corridors of the headquarters, anger and frustration writ large on his face. He had his task cut out and he knew it. The navy's isolation during the 1965 Indo-Pak war had left the sailors deeply demoralized and hurt. Chand knew that any further isolation would not only affect the moral fibre of his men, it would also make them despondent. He was well aware that they were preparing for a war, and felt it was his sole duty to ensure that the navy was not left on the sidelines while the other two services took battle positions and faced the fire. The navy had to be given its rightful place amongst the major actors in this war theatre.

Entering his spacious office, he called his 'ops' team to discuss the burning issue. The team started with the realization that the ground reality had changed since 1965. Having tasted defeat at the hands of India in the 1965 war, Pakistan would now do all it could to inflict damage on the Indian defence forces. In all subsequent meetings with the Defence Minister, RAW's confirmation of the presence of Pakistani submarines, Ghazi, Hangor and Mangro, in Indian waters and the damage they could inflict on Indian pride was repeatedly stressed.

The Defence Minister was a man of foresight and was practical in his approach. He realized the importance of having the navy actively involved.

As the war fever grew stronger, the bureaucracy too realized the far-reaching consequences of undermining Pakistan's intentions. It was soon after that the navy's strategists were given a green signal for their mission 'Bomb Karachi'.

On 1 December 1971, the Indian Navy, for the first time in its history, was issued sealed orders to attack Karachi. The plan was imaginatively drawn on the drawing board. It looked simple on paper but drew its strength from the fact that it was unique, unheard of and untested by any nation in the past naval wars. It had the element of surprise in its armoury which is the first requirement for success.

As per the plan, small missile boats were to be towed up to 200 miles off the Karachi harbour before commencement of the war. These boats were meant for coastal waters only and considered incapable of operating at high seas, even by their sellers, the USSR. These missile boats were launched by the escorting ships when the war broke out on the night of 3 December. Their mission was to hit Karachi harbour and the ships within, and retreat to the mother ships to be towed back to safety.

The first missile attack, 'Operation Trident', was carried out by three missile boats, Veer, Nirghat and Nipat, on the night of 4 December 1971. The resulting devastation shook the Pakistani Navy to its core. Taken by complete surprise, the Pakistani forces suffered heavy casualties and damage. Pakistan's most important and well-protected harbour, Karachi, was rendered non-operational and its naval force disarmed. Most of its shore-based defence batteries were abandoned. The few that remained in action emptied their ammunition, firing in space at non-existent aircraft.

Dumbstruck, the Pakistani intelligence was left struggling, unable to even locate the exact source of attack.

Its frontline destroyer ship, Khaibar, sank without a trace. A nearby oil tanker sank after it caught fire that lasted for over seven days. Shaken by the ingenuity of the attack, the Pakistani Navy panicked. It recalled all its warships to the safety of the harbour, removed all the ammunition to avoid it being blown up and abandoned its naval warfare plans. It thus, unwittingly, gave free passage to the Indian missile boats to return to the safety of Bombay harbour after completing their operation.

A second missile attack on Karachi was carried out by the Indian Navy's frontline ships, Trishul, Talwar and Vinash, on the night of 8 December, destroying Karachi's oil dumps and tankers as well as crippling many ships anchored in the harbour. Pakistan's lack of preparedness could be gauged from the fact that even though its navy was aware of a missile threat, the ship-led attacks were mistaken for an air raid. The ensuing fire blazed for days together, throwing the entire panic-stricken Karachi town into disarray.

News of Ghazi sinking with all hands followed next, leaving the Pakistani high command completely demoralized. On the other hand, the Indian Navy had done its homework rather well. Understanding the fact that Pakistan's main aim was to sink INS Vikrant, the Indian Navy assigned a small destroyer, INS Rajput, whose duty was to patrol the Bay of Bengal and act like it was an aircraft carrier. Lieutenant Commander Sunderjeet Singh, the Commanding Officer of INS Rajput, played his role to perfection by releasing a series of misleading signals intended to waylay the enemy.

From the Bay of Bengal, INS Rajput relayed coded messages of huge LOGREQs (logistics requirements) befitting the size of an aircraft carrier. Messages demanding supplies of 5000 kilos of potatoes, 10,000 kilos of vegetables, 1,00,000 eggs and huge quantities of poultry and meat convinced the Pakistani think tank that it was INS Vikrant sailing in the Bay of Bengal. They were sure that no other ship would need such huge quantities of food supplies.

The entire operation was kept a closely guarded secret, so much so that when the Naval Officer in Madras received immediate demands for unprecedented ration supplies, purportedly from INS Vikrant, he went into a spin and pressed the panic button. Mustering all the men and suppliers under his command, he directed the procurement of all available supply from the market. It was not long before the entire market was abuzz with rumours of the possible arrival of Vikrant at Madras port.

If the Indian Navy's intention was to make the Pakistani spies in Madras believe that INS Vikrant was in the Bay of Bengal, it had hit the bullseye. Months later, documents recovered from the sunken Ghazi carried signals sent by Pakistani headquarters confirming Vikrant's location off the coast of Madras, and directing her to take suitable position on the east coast.

Lieutenant Commander Sunderjeet Singh was a sincere, dedicated officer who, through sheer display of bravery and hard work, had become the Commanding Officer of INS Rajput. During war-room meetings at the Eastern Naval Command Headquarters, he had proposed a daredevil plan to counter the prevailing Ghazi threat.

'Let me take my ship with a limited crew to patrol at the mouth of the harbour. If I sight Ghazi, I shall ram my ship into the submarine when it surfaces to take the final bearing,' he roared. The plan appeared amateurish to most present, but it nevertheless outlined the young Commander's courage to face the jaws of death. Impressed by his raw courage, he was cleared to take his ship out and drop depth charges at different designated spots. These were capable of carpet-bombing underwater and cracking the hull of a submarine by creating substantial water pressure, taking advantage of the fact that most conventional submarines cannot withstand the water pressure at the depth of 200 metres. Such was the desperation to destroy Ghazi.

The next morning, Lieutenant Commander Sunderjeet Singh woke up early. Without disturbing his wife and son, he left the room, showered and changed into his uniform. After fixing the naval crown on his turban, he looked at himself in the mirror. His face was filled with joy and pride. Shortly before leaving home, he entered the prayer room. He closed the door behind him, knelt down and bowed before the holy Granth Sahib. Breaking the silence of the quiet, peaceful morning, Sunderjeet addressed the holy book. 'I am thankful to you for bestowing me with everything. I have one more request to make. Having been assigned this task, please ensure that I either fulfil my duty or do not come back. I will prefer a dignified death than failure.'

Ending his short prayer, Sunderjeet bowed again and stood up to find his wife standing behind him. Her eyes were moist but her face was glowing. His son also peeked naughtily from behind his mother. He didn't understand much but was aware that his father was going for an important mission. His wife offered him prasad. 'May Wahe Guru fulfil your wishes and may you be successful in your mission. I will wait for you . . .' she said as tears streamed down her face.

Sunderjeet thanked his brave wife and hugged her, and then he lifted his son in his arms and kissed him. They stood before the lord one last time and said their prayers.

Sitting in the jeep, he drove off without looking back. Somewhere deep within, not only was he sure of a successful rendezvous with Ghazi, but also of sailing back with his ship's company to tell the tale.

Stepping on board, the cheerful Commanding Officer ordered priming of depth charges to 15 metres depth. The sailors saw a unique look of confidence on his face. They were part of his core team and had volunteered for the mission. By the time INS Rajput left port, the ammunition was primed and ready to be launched. The warship made repeat sorties into the sea, scanning and dropping depth charges in the ocean wherever they saw water bubbles.

While leaving the Vishakhapatnam channel, he noticed heavy churning of the sea at the outer channel. It was an indication of a possible submarine diving into the ocean in a hurry. Directing his ship to that spot, he dropped depth charges and reported to the eastern command before heading into the open sea. Ghazi exploded a few hours later on the night of 4 December 1971 with all hands on board. The shattering explosion could be heard across the harbour. The Pakistani submarine was later identified from its wreckage and flotsam.

The sinking of Ghazi sent panic waves across the Pakistani forces. In addition to a loss of face, it also had a demoralizing effect on the Commander of the forces in eastern Pakistan. Further, its 1,50,000-strong Pakistani troops were cut off from main Pakistan on all sides, including the open sea route. It was not long before the Pakistani intelligentsia realized its folly of falling into the superbly planned Indian trap. But by then irrevocable damage had been done. The Ghazi was an advanced submarine capable of sustained operations for long durations. Its explosion added to the reputation of India's strategic brilliance and lifted the morale of the entire force.

Lieutenant Commander Sunderjeet Singh had indeed achieved what he had set out to do.

20

Successful operations in the Bay of Bengal and the Arabian Sea were filling the Indian Navy's chest with trophies of pride and honour. Meanwhile, another drama was unfolding on the west coast of India. Hangor, the Pakistani submarine, had patiently been waiting for the right target to strike. Having arrived close to the Bombay coast much before the start of the war, it sat on the ocean bed, waiting for the right moment. Hangor had many opportunities to strike at Indian warships leaving Bombay harbour prior to 3 December, but it did not do so for fear of engaging the enemy before the actual commencement of the war. Besides, it also had to ensure its own safe passage from any counter-attack. It thus waited patiently, well aware that Indian ships leaving and entering the harbour were bound to provide it with an opportunity to attack.

Meanwhile, Hangor's movement off the Saurashtra coast in the Arabian Sea was also reported by local fishermen. The Flag Officer Commanding in Chief, Western Naval Command (FOCINC West), had two ships in harbour at that time. INS Kirpan and Khukri were both mid-sized frigates capable of carrying out hunter-killer operations. But Khukri was greatly constrained in hunting operations due to sonar problems and was heavily dependent on its sister ship, the Kirpan, for supply of data on underwater targets. Non-availability of anti-submarine air support further hindered their operation and put the two ships at grave risk of a sub attack.

The Hangor also had the benefit of operating in waters that offered little support to anti-submarine operations. The Arabian Sea is known for its varied temperature gradients. A normal sonar transmission is designed to travel through underwater waves and return after hitting a target, thus indicating the position of the submarine. However, in the Arabian Sea, instead of travelling straight, the variation in the temperature gradient at different levels bends the radio waves downwards, making submarine detection difficult.

The two ships, therefore, faced an uphill task. Their only hope was to physically sight the sub when it surfaced for charging batteries or was in snorkelling mode to send a transmission. Before launching the torpedoes, a submarine needs to lock on to the target in order to set the final bearing in the guidance system of the torpedo. The two ships hoped to catch the transmission before taking evasive actions and engaging counter-attack measures.

But Hangor was already positioned and sitting underwater in passive mode, conserving power and listening with its antennae up. It was a battle loaded in favour of the Pakistani sub from the word go.

Captain Jitendra Kumar, the Commanding Officer of Khukri, was the Squadron Commander of the operation. He knew his limitations, risks and challenges when he received his sailing orders on 8 December 1971. His orders were to set sail in the wee hours along with the sister ship. The two frigates, ships used to protect other ships, Khukri and Kirpan, had about 600 brave officers and sailors. Unlike the Pakistani Navy that had recalled all its ships to the safety of Karachi harbour after the daring attack by Indian missile boats, the two Commanding Officers were keen to take up the challenge even under such adverse conditions.

On the night of 7 December, Captain Kumar stepped out of his house in full battle rig. His wife waited outside while he locked the door. Before sitting in the car, he handed over the house keys to her. 'Take care and wish me luck,' he said softly. There was mystery in his voice. 'And tell the children that I love them.' Taken by surprise at her husband's unusual behaviour, his wife looked closely at his otherwise cheerful face.

'But this is your key. I have mine. And where are we going at this time of the night?'

'Oh, we are dining together at the Taj.'

'Wow! What's the occasion?'

'Every soldier waits his whole life for an opportunity to take on the enemy head-on. That's what we are trained for all our lives. Yet, only a select few get chosen. And by the grace of God, I have been presented with such an opportunity. Thus the celebration.'

His wife was now worried but maintained her composure. She was aware of the ongoing war but also knew her husband too well to protest. They dined in silence, with Captain Kumar making occasional comments on the high morale of his crew. After the meal, he requested to be driven to the outer breakwater where Khukri was berthed. The drive from the hotel to Lion's Gate, the first security checkpoint to the berthing area of the Indian Navy's warships, barely took five minutes.

The Commander-at-Arms was present at the checkpoint since the navy was on the highest state of alert. He peeped into the car and instantly recognized Captain Kumar. Moving a step back and standing to attention, he saluted smartly before bending his head again to face the Commanding Officer.

'I am afraid, Sir, your good lady cannot accompany you to the ship. We are in "Piranha State One" at the moment [immediate state of danger or a war alert].'

'That's okay,' Captain Kumar replied. 'I have a special pass for her.'

The Commander looked at the coloured slip that had been issued by the Admiral's office. Stepping back again, he gave a thumbs up signal to the guard at the far end. A long whistle followed as the barricade began going up, clearing the way for the white vehicle to pass through.

The car drove past the heavily guarded naval dockyard to the outer breakwater where INS Khukri was berthed behind its sister ship, the Kirpan. The Quartermaster standing watch on the forecastle, the front part of the ship, was quick to spot his Commanding Officer's car. He pushed the side pipe in his mouth and blew two short beeps, alerting the Duty Officer and the Coxswain. As the vehicle stopped, the sentry smartly pulled open the rear door and stood aside. Before getting out of the car, Captain Kumar held his wife's hand and looked at her with a smile on his face.

'Don't look back as you leave. It'll make me weak. It is a privilege to serve this great country.'

But she was far from convinced. Khukri was not fully equipped for an anti-submarine operation. She knew this as she had witnessed her husband spending most of his time repeatedly reviewing the status of repair of his ship, even on his short visit home. Pulling herself together and mustering up the courage, she asked, 'But your ship is not fully fit. Are you not rushing it up a bit?'

Captain Kumar was about to step out of the car. Stopping midway, he slid back into the rear seat and shut the door. 'Cursing a flat tyre does not fix it, dear. Things will go wrong. They always do. This is a chance to make the best of what you have. Whether we fail or succeed is not important. It doesn't take great men to do great things, just those who are dedicated to doing them.'

His wife murmured prayers as the car raced up to the quarterdeck of Khukri and turned around to stop abreast of the ship's brow. The sentry ran behind the car and stepped forward to open the door. Captain Kumar emerged from the car and acknowledged salutes of the guards surrounding the ship. Without looking back to even bid goodbye to his wife, he began climbing the gangway. Kumar stood at the end of the gangway till the Quartermasters lowered the side pipes. Bringing his hand down from the saluting position, he hurriedly turned right to look at the tail lights of the departing vehicle that carried his wife. Somewhere deep in his mind, he wondered if he would ever see his wife and children again.

21

Captain Kumar headed straight to the bridge to talk to his Executive Officer (XO).

'XO, are we ready?'

'Yes, Captain. All men on board, ready for sea.'

'Very Good. Remove gangway. Single up all ropes.'

'Aye aye, Captain, single up!' The XO rushed to the starboard wing, lifted both his hands sideways and raised his index finger to the Forecastle and Quarterdeck Officers. Like a well-oiled machine, the many hands on the deck and jetty uncoiled the rope from the bollards, while a small crane on the jetty lifted the gangway and placed it on the tarmac.

'All ropes singled up, gangway removed, Sir,' reported the XO in a crisp and firm tone.

'Very good,' acknowledged the Captain without lifting his eyes from the signal pad which was brought to him by the signal's Yeoman. In the navy, it is mandatory for every order to be repeated by its receiver before implementing the same. It was a practice started by the British Navy centuries ago to avoid miscommunication.

Captain Kumar then turned towards the Engineer Officer (EO) who was standing with the status report of the ship's engines.

'Ready for sea in all respects, Sir.'

'Very good, Chief. I would be needing quick responses from the engine room.'

'Aye aye, Sir,' said the EO before vanishing below the deck.

Captain Kumar glanced at both sides of the wings before sliding into his chair. A coir handle, shackled on the bulkhead, hung loosely in line with his right arm. Captain Kumar slid his fingers around the handle and gripped it firmly to push himself up to take a quick view of the ship in front. Singled up and without the gangway in place, Kirpan was leaving a trail of thin grey smoke from its funnel, in anticipation of casting off at short notice.

'Signal permission to leave harbour.'

'Aye aye, Sir.' The Signal Communication Officer (SCO) looked at his Chief Yeoman. As if on cue, the Yeoman gave a thumbs up signal to the man standing on the bridge top with the semaphore. Minutes later, the two semaphore flags in the man's hands went up and down in rapid succession, sending a visual transmission to the fleet office located at the entrance of the breakwater. Soon after, the SCO came back to Captain Kumar and read a small text from the Fleet Commander.

'From: FOCINC

To: Khukri

Permission granted. Take Kirpan under your command and proceed as previously directed.'

'Very good,' acknowledged the Captain.

'Hold on to the head spring. Let go of all the ropes. Kirpan to cast off and take position in front. Ship's company to remain on "action stations" until further orders.'

'Aye aye, Sir,' acknowledged the XO and pressed the 'action stations' hooter. Relaying the same message to Kirpan in front, he simultaneously took out a whistle from his front pocket and blew a long hoot. The tug master, standing by to pull the ship away from the jetty, moved astern to give room for the ships to manoeuvre. Minutes later, he was again standing in front of the Captain.

'State one executed, Sir. All lines removed, forward spring on. Kirpan told to act as guide ship. Lookouts placed. Depth charges in position.'

'Very good, No. 1,' acknowledged the Captain. Raising his head, he looked at the Officer of the Watch (OOW) and spoke in a polite but crisp tone. 'Slow ahead port.'

It was now the Chief Coxswain's turn to get into action. Holding the wheel firmly with both his hands, he bent towards the voice pipe and repeated the order. The OOW simultaneously pulled back the right lever on the engine room repeater.

The engine-room team sprang into action, acknowledged the order through the voice pipe and set the right propeller into motion. The ship moved ahead initially but stopped because of the forward spring. As a result, it swung left and the rear of the ship (quarterdeck) moved away from the jetty. The ship's nose was now almost touching the jetty. Maintaining his composure and keeping his eyes on Kirpan that had also begun to move astern, the Captain waved his hand. 'Let go forward spring.'

'Let go forward spring,' repeated the XO. Anticipating the order, the XO had already raised his hands in the air. Flapping them once, he recalled the only line that was keeping the ship attached to the jetty. Without waiting for the Forecastle Officer to confirm compliance, the XO turned towards the Captain yet again.

'All lines on board, Captain. Ship's under way.'

'Very good. Stop port. Slow astern both engines. Starboard fifteen.'

Both the OOW and the Coxswain repeated their part of the order as the ship picked up speed, moving astern.

'Both engines going slow astern, fifteen of starboard wheel on, Sir,' said the Quartermaster.

'Very good. Midships.'

'Midships,' came the reply as the big wheel swung back to its centre position.

'Both engines going slow astern, wheel at midship, Sir.'

From the port wing, the Navigating Officer (NO) visually checked the distance from the Middle Ground Coastal Battery. He looked at Captain Kumar and then at the closing distance between the ship and the middle ground where the ship was slowly heading. There were no traces of worry on his face, though. Having sailed with Kumar many times before, he knew the capabilities of his Commanding Officer only too well.

'Stop both engines,' he heard the Captain order. As if put on brakes, the ship slowed instantly. He smiled in admiration at the quick response of the engine-room team. Working mostly through manual controls, the engine-room staff had to be exceptionally trained to receive orders, acknowledge them and pass them further down to the engine room for it to be executed in the shortest period of time.

'All yours, pilot, keep her behind Kirpan,' the Captain said, without moving from his chair.

'Aye aye, Captain,' acknowledged the NO. He then bent forward and announced into the voice pipe, 'Slow ahead both engines.' Without waiting for an acknowledgement from the engine room, he took the final bearings before steering the ship in the desired direction.

Both propellers began churning water simultaneously, pushing the ship forward. The middle ground battery that the ship was threatening to hit a short while ago, began falling behind. Minutes later, the two ships were under way, leaving Bombay harbour for their first ever hunter-killer operation.

Despite being a junior ship, Kirpan acted as the guide. It had operational sonar, the only equipment between the two ships capable of detecting the enemy hiding beneath the sea. The sonar team sent underwater transmissions and maintained a strict vigil. The crew knew that it was no friendly exercise. Even a single miss could send their ship to 'Davy Jones's Locker', a term commonly used by seafarers for the bottom of the ocean. The sonar team also realized that in case of a torpedo attack, their chances of survival were at best remote.

With headphones glued to their ears, they watched the large green sonar screen that continuously scanned the ocean. Lieutenant Commander Rana, the Torpedo Anti-Submarine (TAS) Officer, was an experienced hand, having done hundreds of similar exercises. Listening to the echo of the returning signal, he could even make out the nature of the underwater obstruction. Despite the ship being in 'action stations', he was not wearing the mandatory life jacket. 'It gives confidence to my boys,' he maintained. With his eyes partially closed, he focused intently on listening to the sound of the echoes, based on which he kept pressing the 'all clear' signal to the bridge.

In reality though, danger was not far away. Hangor was an advanced French Daphne-class modern submarine. Equipped with sophisticated gadgets and sensors, it was capable of detecting targets much before frigates could even become aware of its presence. Moving at a depth of 50 metres, it closely monitored the search pattern of the two patrolling warships and realized that they were carrying out a rectangular anti-submarine search. Anticipating their movements, Hangor manoeuvred to position itself to attack. At 1900 hours on 9 December, it was all set to launch its torpedoes.

At 1915 hours, the Commanding Officer of Hangor sounded battle stations. A short while later, he brought the sub to periscope depth but could not see the ships. It was a moonless night. Even though the frigates were unaware of the submarine being so close, as a safety measure, they maintained complete blackout and were difficult to sight. Hangor dived to a depth of 50 metres and made a sonar approach in order to lock on to the target. It fired the first homing torpedo at 1957 hours at a depth of 40 metres. The torpedo was tracked by the Hangor crew for a few tension-filled moments but no explosion was heard. The torpedo went past Kirpan without exploding.

Meanwhile, on the Kirpan, Lieutenant Commander Rana jumped from his seat. The sound of the echo was loud and clear. Years of training and experience told him what it was. Holding the mike firmly in his hand, he shouted, 'Torpedo, torpedo, torpedo, 240 degrees, close range.' But before the two ships could even break the search pattern, the torpedo had already gone past Kirpan without exploding. Khukri was stationed on the port of Kirpan. Instead of moving away from the submarine's line of attack, Kumar decided to go for the kill. At that time, Khukri was doing twelve knots. It took some time for the engine room to provide her with full power. And this delay proved fatal.

The Hangor, being in a tactically advantageous position, launched the second torpedo at 2012 hours. Khukri was within range and moving at medium speed, thus offering an opportunity that couldn't be missed. The torpedo travelled for five long minutes before it hit its target in the magazine compartment, blowing the ammunition hold and almost breaking the ship into two. Khukri sank within two minutes of taking the hit.

Captain Kumar, sitting firmly in his chair, ordered 'abandon ship' but refused to leave his post. As Khukri began to sink, he visualized the tail lights of his wife's car leaving the outer breakwater. He was a brave man and wore no traces of fear. Firmly gripping the armrests of the chair, he murmured, 'Goodbye, dear, *ab hum toh safar karte hein* [I'm moving on].'

INS Khukri sank at about 2019 hours, killing eighteen officers and 176 sailors. But Hangor was far from done. Even though it was in an extremely vulnerable position, it fired a third torpedo at Kirpan before fleeing to deeper waters. Kirpan outran the torpedo and later turned back to the sinking Khukri to rescue six officers and sixty-one sailors who survived to tell the tale. Having lost precious time in picking up the survivors, she was in no position to launch a counter-attack on the fleeing submarine.

For the next four days and nights, Hangor evaded extensive search and counter-attacks of over 150 underwater projectiles and depth charges, but somehow managed to keep itself at a safe distance. On 18 December 1971, she entered Karachi harbour safe and unharmed. Having lost their flag submarine Ghazi and a host of other ships to the daring Indian Navy attack, Pakistan had managed to salvage some pride.

22

Tej located an old haveli in Maler Kotla. Aby pitched in and got it renovated quickly so that Sehmat could shift to her new home directly from the hospital. Even though the new town was dramatically different from the quiet, serene, cool and picturesque surroundings of her home in Srinagar, Tej was happy to fulfil her only child's wishes. She went a step further and sold off all her assets and businesses in Kashmir to become a permanent resident of Maler Kotla.

While Mir got busy with the impending war, Tej began her efforts to rejuvenate Sehmat and nurse her back to health. But the more Tej tried to cheer her up, the deeper Sehmat sank into depression. She soon became unaware of her surroundings and remained huddled within the confines of the four walls of her room. For Tej, it was extremely distressing to see her daughter, who would once jump in ecstasy at the sight of a butterfly, now sitting in the corner of her room, ignoring life and staring into space.

With the passage of time, Sehmat withdrew from all activities of normal life. She also steadfastly declined to be honoured by the government for her services to the nation and, instead, preferred to live in isolation and seclusion. Her guilt entrapped her like a vice and refused to let go. Tej's only hope was the child that Sehmat was soon to deliver, but even that failed to bring cheer to her. Sehmat delivered a healthy, cherubic boy, but far from feeling good, she now saw herself as his father's murderer and refused to attend to the newborn.

Unnerved by the disturbing past that flashed through her mind every now and then, Sehmat began hallucinating. Abdul's blood-soaked face stared down at her menacingly. The sound of his bones getting crushed under the wheels of the army truck began to haunt her. She dreaded going to sleep. Consequently, instead of taking care of her child and basking in motherhood, she became hysterical. It was Aby who once again came to the rescue. He not only adopted the child but also shifted him to Delhi, thus keeping the newborn away from Sehmat. Against the wishes of Tej, he named him Samar Khan. 'I have adopted the child,' he argued, 'but I have no right to change his religion.'

Aby could feel his heart shatter into a million fragments as he drove Samar from Maler Kotla to Delhi. Holding the gurgling baby close to him, he whispered emotionally, 'You will grow up to be a wonderful human being. You are your mother's pride and joy. It's only that she is a broken person right now. Never hold it against her, Samar. You have no idea what a remarkable woman your mother is. Till then, we have each other.'

Days turned into weeks, and weeks into months and years but Sehmat's condition did not improve. The initial hysteria gave way to a calm acceptance and deadly indifference. She was polite to anyone she unwillingly met, yet remained detached from the outside world. The worried mother in Tej had almost given up hope of Sehmat's recovery, till one day a miracle took place. For Sehmat, it was a regular day like any other. In her room with her mother, she, as usual, did not notice the gregarious twittering of the birds outside her house.

The sky was overcast with thick clouds, promising rain. Suddenly, the birds that routinely gathered at Sehmat's window flew away in all directions. The two friendly street dogs, who had once found their way into the haveli and were now part of the family, started barking ferociously, as if to chase away a stranger.

A fakir, a nomad stood in front of the haveli. Dressed in a tattered black gown, his beard long and unkempt, he was singing hymns from holy books. Sehmat's room was on the first floor. She was sitting listlessly on the floor while Tej, sitting on a chair, was massaging her head. Sehmat's eyes lit up as she heard the singing. She listened for a few moments and asked Tej to stop. Then, suddenly, she sprang up and bolted out of the room at lightning speed, her hair flying behind her. Taken aback by Sehmat's unexpected behaviour, Tej attempted to follow her in panic. By then, Sehmat's youthful legs had carried her to the door. Tej watched her in utter disbelief. There was urgency in Sehmat's expressions and an inexplicable excitement in her eyes.

Sehmat held the banister briefly and ran down the wooden stairs, jumping two steps at a time, her right hand effortlessly gliding over the railing. On reaching the last step, she paused briefly before lunging towards the main door and flinging it open.

The fakir was still standing there, as if waiting for the door to open. His eyes were shut, oblivious to the storm he had stirred in the Khan household. He continued singing in praise of the Almighty. His face was partially hidden by his long, dusty beard. His clothes were torn. His body bore injuries caused by stones that street children threw at him every day. He held a small musical instrument in his right hand that played in unison between his fingers to the beat of the hymns. His melodious voice had enormous depth, enough to electrify the soul. His lyrics spoke of a man who had seen the world in all its myriad hues. But his appearance was scary enough to keep people away.

Sehmat watched him for a few moments before sitting down on the steps of the haveli. Shutting her eyes, she rested her head against the wall and listened intently to the hymns. Tej was shocked by the sudden change in her daughter's behaviour. She stood at the doorstep and looked at the stranger. After a brief moment, the fakir stopped singing and turned his gaze towards the women.

'Can you give me some water, please?' he said and extended his left hand. A container slid from his palm until its thin handle nestled on his fingertips.

'Yes, yes of course. Please come in,' Tej said and moved away from the entrance, even though she was unsure of her decision.

It was now the fakir's turn to be surprised. 'Are you sure that I should come in?'

'Yes, of course. You must be a noble soul, for it is the first time in a very long time that my daughter has shown any kind of excitement.'

'Strange. Very strange. The entire village hates me and hurls stones along with the choicest abuses at me. And here we have a lady who invites me into her home. Are you not scared of the wrath of the villagers? You must know that I am considered a bad omen by the whole village.'

Tej noticed a mysterious smile on the fakir's face. She felt stressed and frightened.

Before Tej could reply, Sehmat opened her eyes and looked at the fakir. Her face displayed a sense of urgency, as if she would miss a train if the fakir did not resume his singing. Her hands were stretched open in excitement and every part of her body was filled with new-found life.

'Please don't stop. Can you sing more?'

Tej's face lit up with happiness. It was the first time Sehmat had shown interest in anything around her since her return to India. Her voice was pleading, urging the fakir to sing.

The fakir looked at Sehmat and smiled. He carefully surveyed the surroundings and then, without uttering a word, walked to the other end of the hall and stopped in front of a wall which had a picture of Lord Krishna. He put his instrument and container down and sat on the floor with his back towards the two women. The servant rushed in with a tray holding a jug of water and two glasses. He too looked bemused to see the village outcast sitting comfortably inside the haveli.

Tej filled the glass with water and offered it to the fakir. He looked up and accepted the glass but said nothing. He then gulped the water in one go and gestured at Tej to sit on the floor. She did as she was told but Sehmat kept standing, eagerly waiting for him to sing again.

'You should pray, lady . . .' the fakir began. 'This place is worthy of becoming a temple. You'll see your daughter become hale and hearty very soon. There will be happiness in your life once again. She has a kind heart. Her mind suffers from unfortunate developments, but by the grace of God, she'll recover soon.'

Tej was in a quandary about taking him seriously. She had seen an umpteen number of soothsayers in her life, who had scammed their way to riches. His looks and attire did not inspire confidence either. But the doubt in her mind instantly vanished when the fakir completed his next sentence. 'And then you would be able to bring your grandson home.'

Tej's eyes widened with surprise and excitement. But before she could react, the fakir picked up his instrument and began singing again, much to Sehmat's delight. His song beckoned her to a world where selflessness and sacrifice ruled supreme, where love conquered hatred, where humanity was the biggest truth, and universal brotherhood the only religion. Sehmat listened to him with rapt attention and continued sitting at the same spot for hours even after he left the haveli.

She repeatedly hummed the lines that spoke of forgiveness, reflecting at the same time on whether she had really forgiven herself. The fakir visited every day thereafter and sang for Sehmat before vanishing into the dusty lanes of the crowded Maler Kotla. His spiritual songs worked like a magic potion, helping Sehmat improve with each passing day. She began to sleep well and her occasional laughter filled both Tej's heart and the haveli's teak walls with hope and joy.

Tej was no longer apprehensive about the fakir and converted the living room into a prayer hall. Seeing Sehmat's miraculous recovery, neighbours too started joining in for these early morning prayers. The fakir now had a small following of people who accompanied him through the streets, singing with him. Both Tej and Sehmat made it a point to receive the group at their doorstep each day and serve them tea and snacks in the veranda.

Though the change came slowly, it made its presence felt. It was a bright early morning. The rays of the sun were breaking the cover of darkness and entering Sehmat's bedroom through the large glass windowpanes. Sitting motionless, Sehmat was engrossed in meditation, trying hard to focus inwards. Her interaction with the fakir had brought her out of deep depression. She was beginning to put her nightmarish past behind her. Abdul's face had faded from her memory to an extent that it no longer haunted her. The glow on her face was returning, encouraging Sehmat to accept life and its gifts.

She abruptly opened her eyes and widened them as if awakened from deep slumber. Looking from left to right, she found nothing unusual but her heart did not agree with what she saw. She realized somebody had interrupted her meditation. She stood up, rushed out of her room and started walking down the stairs. Her eyes eagerly looked around, searching for the intruder. She waited briefly at the last step of the wooden stairs, gripping the banister with her right hand. Mustering her courage, she walked to the front door and pulled it open.

In front of her was a familiar face. He was dressed in a sparkling white robe. His face was glowing; his hair was combed backwards and tied neatly in a ponytail. His hands were folded close to his chest. His feet were bare but did not have even a speck of dust on them. Spellbound, Sehmat looked at the visitor's face. The fakir was smiling mysteriously.

Stepping aside, Sehmat let him in and walked behind him like a dutiful disciple to the end of the hall which, over time, had become the fakir's seating area. She waited till the fakir turned and sat on the floor and then sat at a short distance from him. There was no trace of fear or suspense on her face, but her eyes were inquisitive. As if prompted from deep within, Sehmat then broke the silence.

23

'How do I find peace? I have sinned, committed unpardonable crimes. It haunts me,' Sehmat asked, impatience writ large on her forehead.

Without exchanging any pleasantries, the fakir began softly, 'Be in touch with your soul if you desire peace. Your soul is peaceful, serene and wonderful, like the rays of the sun. The light [aura] is so brilliant! Everything comes from this light! Energy comes from this light. It's almost like a magnetic force that we are attracted to. It's like a power source. It knows how to heal. Conflict is natural. It is not necessarily a disease to be cured or a disorder to be curbed. It may even be necessary to some extent as it opens up opportunities for learning.'

'How do I reach this state?'

'Travelling is a great experience by itself. And when you have open skies and barren land to communicate with, you learn about the world and everything beyond it. You had a mission in your own heart. You thus opted to travel in the chosen path. After accomplishing your goals, you began to ponder about the right and wrong. The resultant analysis put you in deep depression. By His grace, you are back to normal. But that's not what you want. You now wish to travel where few dare.'

'And will I be able to reach where I wish to?' Sehmat's voice was barely audible to even herself. She was murmuring, as if talking to herself. The fakir was at complete peace with himself, yet alert, picking up every whisper.

'The Upanishads say, when you are inspired by some great purpose, some extraordinary project, all your thoughts break their bonds, your mind transcends limitations, your consciousness expands in every direction and you find yourself in a new, great and wonderful world. Dominant forces, faculties and talents come alive and you find yourself to be a bigger person than you'd ever dreamed.' He continued, 'The knowledge of happiness also brings with it unhappiness. Materialism leads to misery. Therefore we must shed greed and stay simple and contented. This is the law. And this is maya.

'Every child is born with dreams. As he grows he carries this energy of dreams with him. He is so full of youth that it is hard for him to believe that there is such a thing as death, such a thing as defeat or degradation. It's only when old age comes and starts the decline of the body that he becomes aware of death.

'Our progress, our vanities, our reforms, our luxuries, our wealth, our knowledge have that one end, death. Cities come and go, empires rise and fall, planets break into pieces and crumble into dust. Death is the end of everything. Death is the end of life, beauty, wealth, power and virtue, too. Saints die and so do sinners; kings and beggars are destined to meet the same fate. Everything around us—the stars, the planets, the moon—is moving at a defined pace and is destined to die. And yet there is this tremendous urge to cling to life. Somehow, we find it difficult to give up. And that is maya.'

'Do we choose the time and place of our birth and death? Can we choose our situation?' Sehmat's interest in his words was growing deeper. She urged him with her eyes to go on.

'Yes, we know when we have accomplished what we were sent down here to accomplish. We know when the time is up and will accept death when it comes. For you know that you can get nothing more out of this lifetime. When you have had the time to rest and re-energize your soul, you are allowed to choose your re-entry back into the physical state.'

'How do we select the right path?'

'Everybody's path is basically the same. We must all learn to be charitable, give hope, have faith, share love—follow the path of the lord while we are in our physical state. Some of us are quicker to accept and learn than the others. It's not just one hope and one faith and one love. Those who follow the path do not seek returns. They know that following the path has its own returns. While the rest of us, more involved in the worldly pleasures, look for rewards and justifications.

'You must eradicate all fears from your mind. Fear is a waste of energy. It stifles you from fulfilling what you were sent here to fulfil. Fear can't reach your soul. And that is where we must strive to reach.'

'How?' Sehmat was now in deep meditation, barely murmuring, grabbing every word being uttered by the master soul.

'Have you seen a mountain? It looks calm and solid from the outside but within it contains the volcano, the energy. Humans can only see the outside, but that alone is not the truth. The truth is also the inside, so you need to go much deeper. You have to see the volcano. To be only on the physical plane is not the natural state of being as we all imagine. The most natural state of being is being in a spiritual state.'

The fakir's voice was steady, his body in a relaxed frame. Except for his lips, everything else was still, peaceful and serene.

'Is learning faster in the physical state or in the spiritual state? Is there any reason why everyone doesn't stay in the spiritual state which, as you say, is the natural state of being?'

'People don't stay in the spiritual state because they are pulled by maya. They think that is the only truth. They don't realize that what is pulling them is just the physical world which is only an instrument to get to the spiritual state.'

Sehmat processed the information in her mind. What had happened with her and those connected with her was because of her karma, her actions. They had led her to this state and the solution was to seek spiritual answers. For a few minutes, she stayed absolutely still and calm.

She knew what she had to do. She began replaying what had happened to her in the past couple of years in her mind. This time she was fearless. When she woke up from her meditation, bright and clear, the fakir was nowhere to be seen.

* * *

The fakir's prophecy came true yet again: Sehmat inquired about her son the next morning. Exclaiming with joy, Tej ran to the nearest phone and hurriedly called Aby. In her excitement she didn't notice the panchayat meeting that was taking place not too far from the haveli.

Liyaqat Ali, the village head, was addressing a gathering of Muslim clerics and village elders assembled under the huge tree outside his house. He stood on the raised ground around the tree that had over the years become a platform for the panchayat leader to address the gathering. 'This fakir is making our religion look insignificant and irrelevant. Going by his hymns and songs, I am not even sure if he is a Muslim. His growing popularity is an even bigger concern. He perhaps has knowledge of black magic with which he is influencing the masses. I am afraid if we do nothing to stop his antics, he will become a major threat to our people.'

Ali stopped briefly to see the reaction of his audience, knowing fully well that most of them did not have the courage to oppose him. The clerics were by now shaking their heads in agreement, urging Ali to continue his speech. 'And then there is this new family of half Hindus that is encouraging this fakir and his disciples. I am telling my son, Salim, and his friends to suitably warn them once, failing which they would be responsible for their own safety.'

Ali's threat wasn't taken lightly by those present. His son was a known goon of the area and feared for the viciousness with which he had eliminated his father's opponents in the past. Ali also enjoyed excellent relations with the local cops. It was a give and take arrangement, where the cops collected fixed sums every month for turning a blind eye to his son's illegal activities.

He jumped down from the platform on a triumphant note and walked up to his son. Holding him by his shoulder,

Ali turned him towards the crowd, gently thrusting him forward like a well-earned trophy. 'I direct my son to take care of things for the benefit of our society, for our religion!' He then turned towards the clerics sitting in the front row and smiled before walking towards his house.

An hour later, Salim, together with his handful of toughies, was knocking at the haveli door.

24

Mir was holding the receiver and listening attentively to the one-sided conversation. His only contribution was a series of 'hmm . . .' that he emitted at regular intervals. From his face, however, it was clear that he was engaged in something very serious. After a long pause and silence on both sides, Mir spoke in a crisp and firm tone before ending the conversation. 'Get them all. Confirm post-haste.'

'Yes, Sir,' came a short reply. Replacing the receiver, he called for his assistant. 'I want to leave for Maler Kotla right now!'

The assistant was an old hand. Having worked with Mir for over a decade, he could read his boss's mind like the back of his hand. He could sense the urgency in Mir's tone. Maler Kotla was special and he knew why. Nodding, he vanished into the privacy of his cubicle and pressed into action the various instruments kept on his table. He dialled a few numbers and deftly synchronized the events that were to unfold later.

On behalf of his boss, he summoned officers of varied ranks and profiles. He knew exactly who was needed and at what time. Minutes later, he was back in Mir's room.

'Sir, the air force will provide you the necessary sortie at two hours' notice. I have confirmed your departure for 1500 hours, two hours from now.' Without waiting for his boss to acknowledge the details, the PA continued, 'Our division heads will receive you at the site. I have asked area police heads to reach the site as well. The Assistant Commissioner of Police will be present too. The ACP sounded confused, though, and wanted to know the agenda in advance. A special team is also being dispatched to carry out raids at the designated places.'

'Thanks.' Mir's reply was short and curt. One could not tell if he was impressed with his PA's performance or not.

A few hours later, Mir's helicopter was hovering over the outskirts of Maler Kotla before landing on the makeshift helipad. Mir came out covering his eyes, protecting them from the dust churned by the rotating blades. As soon as he was clear of the range of the rotor blades, the chopper took off, leaving him and his two deputies in the company of nervous officials. Most in the receiving party had never seen a helicopter land at such close quarters. In awe of Mir's official status and gripped by an unknown fear, they began trembling in their shoes as soon as they stepped forward to shake hands with him.

After exchanging pleasantries, Mir sat in a white car fitted with a red beacon on its hood. A pilot jeep was positioned in front with armed guards protecting the motorcade. Led by a screaming siren, the vehicles sped away, leaving behind overwhelmed farmers and a trail of dust.

Half an hour later, Mir was sitting across from a group of officials who were still clueless about the reason behind his visit. He looked at them carefully, maintaining a stern face. The District Collector (DC), being the most senior in the hierarchy, sat nearest to Mir. He was holding a pen and a bunch of loose paper sheets, like a steno waiting for dictation. All the others sat in front of him, wearing blank expressions and searching each other's face for clues.

'Are you the area in-charge?' Mir's first pointed question took the police official by surprise.

'Yes . . . err, yes, Sir, I am. My name is Sanjay Narula, Sir. I am the ACP.'

'Tell me about Sub-Inspector Munnawar Hussein.' There was unmistakable anger in Mir's voice that wasn't missed by anyone in the room.

The ACP was dumbstruck and stammered briefly. He wondered what Munnawar had done to shake the Delhi high offices to such an extent. He was also scared deep inside as he too was a recipient of the ill-gotten wealth that the sub-inspector (SI) had amassed.

'Sir, he is an ordinary SI, just does his job and maintains law and order. I have not received any complaints against him. In fact, the villagers seem happy with him and have generally shown satisfaction with his day-to-day functioning.'

'Have you ever interacted with the villagers personally?'

The ACP was taken aback again. He was now certain that Munnawar was involved in something serious that could put his career in jeopardy. His sixth sense told him to stick to bare facts and somehow save his own skin.

'No, Sir, I have not. But I do regularly check the records. And it shows that the crime graph has not risen.'

'How will the crime graph rise when there aren't any records? No registers, no logbooks, nothing whatsoever?'

'Sir, I . . . err, I mean, Sir, I . . . will err check . . . and revert, Sir.'

'Check what, when? You may wait outside. I'll call for you shortly,' Mir said curtly. His eyes were bristling with anger, as he dismissed the ACP from the room.

'Yes, Sir,' said the ACP as he hurriedly stood up and saluted before making an exit. He was perplexed and wished to speak to Munnawar urgently to ascertain the facts and prepare his own defence.

Pacing up and down the corridor, he was still brainstorming when he noticed all the officials emerging from the room in quick succession. Only the DC remained inside with Mir. The two spent another ten minutes together before emerging. They headed straight to their respective cars. Mir did not even bother to look at the ACP. The waiting officials also rushed to their respective vehicles. The DC positioned his car behind the pilot jeep, leading the motorcade towards Maler Kotla. Sitting alone in his car and holding a walkie-talkie over his ears, he continued to pass orders till the motorcade stopped outside the police chowki of Maler Kotla.

The chowki was in a shambles and looked like an old stable. There were two cows and three buffaloes inside the compound, merrily grazing on the wild grass and hay. The board outside the chowki was hanging upside down. Dozens of rusted bicycles were lying to the left of the gate, piled on top of each other in a small mountain of collected junk. A few cots lay haphazardly under a large tree surrounded by heaps of dry leaves. From the look of it, one could not be sure if there was anyone inside the police chowki.

The scene inside was no better. Sub-Inspector Munnawar Hussein was in a state of deep slumber, unaware of the trouble he was about to get into. An empty liquor bottle lay in front of him. His eyes were half shut, his mouth partially open, the sound of snores filtering through his betel-stained lips. His shirt was open, hanging loosely on both sides of his naked belly that moved up and down with his loud snores. His shoes lay upside down nearby. The table was stacked with numerous files. Like a heavy paperweight, his feet were resting on top of them.

The constable on duty was in no state to raise an alarm either. Having polished his share of the local brew, he too was fast asleep with his head resting squarely on the attendance register. An empty glass and a broken bottle were lying on the floor, with pieces of glass scattered beneath the table. His trousers were wet with splotches of liquor. His belt was unhooked and hanging aimlessly, swaying like a pendulum in sync with the movement of his pot belly.

Mir entered first, followed by the rest of the officials. The ACP was the last to step in and desperately muttered curses on Munnawar Hussein. His fate was sealed and he knew it well. Files, dirty teacups and utensils were scattered all across the room which wore a dilapidated look. There were cobwebs on every wall. The lock-up rooms were ajar, and dirty linen hung haphazardly on a thin wire. There were no sentries in sight but the board on the wall displayed an 'on duty: 6' sign.

Mir glanced around and reached for the attendance register that was lying on the constable's table. The thick book was doubling as the constable's pillow. His head went up as Mir pulled the notebook out and slammed it on the table. The wooden table emitted a loud thud but that failed to wake up the constable. Mir flipped through the register, then turned towards the ACP and flung the book at him. The ACP had to dive to catch the thick, fluttering register.

Holding it in his hand, he glanced at the blank pages. There were no entries in the book for over a month. He faced Mir sheepishly, not knowing where to look. 'I am sorry, Sir . . .' was all that he could manage.

'Sorry for what? For filling your own coffers with the help of this character or for abetting crime and terrorizing people in the name of law? Take these jokers into custody and have this post suitably manned. Take pictures of this police station in this condition and make a detailed report of all this. Send it to your headquarters first thing tomorrow morning, with a copy to the DC,' thundered Mir, sending shivers down the ACP's spine.

'Yes, Sir,' came the meek reply. Like a frozen fish, the ACP continued to stare at the register. The pages were blank but he could clearly imagine his own suspension order written on it in bold ink. Mir stepped out of the chowki on hearing the sound of an approaching vehicle. An officer in plain clothes jumped out of the car and stood to attention in front of him.

'Sir, all have been arrested, including the father and the son. They have been taken for interrogation. The raid has also resulted in the recovery of illicit liquor, arms and munitions. The haveli has been damaged from inside and is in a bad shape. Mrs Tej is wounded, but her condition is stable. She has been admitted to the hospital and is receiving medical attention. Mrs Sehmat Khan had a miraculous escape. She is with her mother right now.' After delivering his statement like a well-rehearsed dialogue, the official waited for Mir's response.

Mir heaved a momentary sigh of relief on hearing about Sehmat's well-being. 'What about Mrs Tej? How serious is she?'

'Sir, the doctors are examining her. There's no serious injury but she may need to be shifted to a better hospital for special care.'

'And how has Sehmat taken it? Is she doing well? How did she escape the attack?' Mir's angry, tense face was beginning to relax a bit.

The official continued, 'It was a miracle, Sir. I hear that a god-man also reached the spot with his followers at almost the same time and confronted the attackers inside the haveli. While Mrs Tej Khan stood at the staircase, letting the attackers damage the property at will, this god-man stood firmly between Mrs Sehmat Khan and the attackers and did not let them climb to the first floor where she was resting. I understand that she was meditating behind closed doors. Amazingly, she did not even hear the commotion and appeared calm on learning about the damage caused by the goons. In fact, she is practically in-charge at the hospital and is even directing the doctors and nurses. She's in high spirits and in full control.'

'Thanks. Please take us to the hospital.' Mir was now sounding relaxed. His face had a look of relief and happiness.

The official jumped on to the front seat and did as he was told. Mir sat behind and the motorcade again sped to its new destination, leaving behind a crowd of spectators who had gathered outside the police station. Their faces lit up with joy on seeing a handcuffed Munnawar Hussein and his deputy getting shoved into the waiting van. The villagers kept standing there even after the dust generated by the speeding cars had settled. The truth of Munnawar Hussein's arrest was taking time to sink in.

An old man watched the proceedings from a distance. There was pain in his eyes. He had repeatedly failed to lodge a complaint against Liyaqat Ali and his son, even as the two goons had forcibly occupied his small piece of land and mercilessly beaten up his wife and son. It was as if Munnawar's arrest had given him a new lease of life. He kept his walking stick aside and began to clap. His weak hands could barely meet, but his face did enough to electrify the atmosphere.

Soon the spectators joined in and began applauding in unison. As if waiting for an opportune moment, the clouds too burst open. By now, the villagers had gathered in large numbers. The applause turned into a roar and the roar into an impromptu dance. Their tears merged with the raindrops that fell rapidly on their faces. The sound of thunder could do little to match their spirited cheering. They were crying with joy and relief at the same time. The rain dance continued, encouraging hundreds of feet to jump in ecstasy and splash the water that was falling straight from the heavens. There was just one person who looked sad and depressed. Holding his head in shame, the ACP walked past the dancing crowd and melted into the distance.

Far away from the crowd, the fakir stood all by himself under a tree. His face was expressionless. His eyes were half shut but the instrument in his hand was playing to an unsung tune. 'It's all due to Sehmat Bi. Go, thank her,' he said repeatedly. His words did not reach the crowd that was becoming more and more ecstatic and emotional. But the villagers wasted no time in grasping the truth. Sehmat was their saviour. She had descended from the heavens to give them respite from the terror they had lived in. She was to be the queen of Maler Kotla.

Epilogue

Gaurav Ghei and his wife Anjali were ordered to leave Pakistan soon after their arrest.

General Sayeed committed suicide instead of facing a court martial. He shot himself in the head inside his haveli.

Sarfraz Khan went missing for many months. His body was later fished out of a canal near Lahore.

Tejashwari Khan (Tej) passed away a few years after her daughter. Her remains were laid to rest next to her beloved daughter, Sehmat Khan.

Samar Khan quit the Indian Army prematurely and began working for an NGO, focusing on the development and holistic growth of underserved and underprivileged children, especially around Maler Kotla.

Abhinav, Aby, did not marry and continues to support his foster son, Samar, in fulfilling Sehmat's dreams.

Acknowledgements

I would like to thank the following people:
My parents for their blessings.
Mr Ajay G. Piramal for being a solid pillar all through.
My family for being a great support.
Admiral S.M. Nanda for his book, *The Man Who Bombed Karachi, A Memoir.*